# JOSHU
# SON

# JOAN HIATT HARLOW

# JOSHUA'S SONG

MARGARET K. McELDERRY BOOKS

NEW YORK  LONDON  TORONTO  SYDNEY  SINGAPORE

# ALSO BY JOAN HIATT HARLOW
## STAR IN THE STORM

—⚓—

Margaret K. McElderry Books
An imprint of Simon & Schuster Children's Publishing Division
1230 Avenue of the Americas
New York, New York 10020

Book design by Michael Nelson
Map by Kristan J. Harlow
The text of this book is set in Lomba Book.

Printed in the United States of America
2 4 6 8 10 9 7 5 3 1

LIBRARY OF CONGRESS CATALOGING-IN-PUBLICATION DATA
Harlow, Joan Hiatt.
Joshua's song / Joan Hiatt Harlow.
p. cm.
Summary: Needing to earn money after his father's death during the influenza
epidemic of 1918, thirteen-year-old Joshua works as a newspaper boy in Boston,
one day finding himself in the vicinity of an explosion that sends
tons of molasses coursing through the streets.
ISBN 0-689-84119-1
[1. Newspaper carriers—Fiction. 2. Child labor—Fiction.
3. Disasters—Fiction. 4. Molasses—Fiction.
5. Boston (Mass.)—Fiction.] I. Title.
PZ7.H22666 Jo 2002
[Fic]—dc21
00-052537

FIRST
EDITION

To Richard Lee Harlow,
my husband, my helper, my hero

# CONTENTS

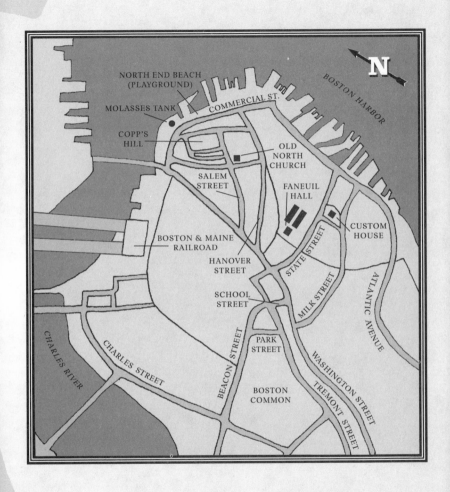

NORTH END BEACH
(PLAYGROUND)

MOLASSES TANK

COPP'S
HILL

COMMERCIAL ST.

BOSTON HARBOR

N

OLD
NORTH
CHURCH

SALEM
STREET

FANEUIL
HALL

CUSTOM
HOUSE

BOSTON & MAINE
RAILROAD

HANOVER
STREET

STATE STREET

MILK STREET

ATLANTIC AVENUE

SCHOOL
STREET

CHARLES RIVER

CHARLES STREET

BEACON STREET

PARK
STREET

WASHINGTON STREET

TREMONT STREET

BOSTON
COMMON

BOSTON, c. 1919

# JOSHUA'S
# SONG

# JOB JITTERS

THE SOUND OF CREAKING WAGON WHEELS AND clinking bottles broke through Joshua's dreams. Was it dawn already? The milkman's horse neighed softly in the alley beneath the window.

Joshua yawned and stretched in the small brass bed. His room wasn't heated, and the January morning was cold. His mother was already clattering pans in the kitchen. Before the Spanish Influenza struck the family several months ago, things had been different. Every morning his mother used to sleep late while Annie, the housekeeper, brought coffee and toast up to the big bedroom. Dad would be shaving and humming in the bathroom. Joshua's morning had been full of his father's singing, his mother's soft laughter when Dad teased her from her sleep, and the smell of coffee.

That was before that awful day—the day Joshua's father died from the virulent pneumonia that was part of the influenza. Just when it seemed that the whole family would recover, Joshua's dad lost his fight. The flu epidemic had taken another victim.

Mom didn't laugh anymore. Instead, she cried late at night and banged the pots and pans early in the morning.

Two weeks ago, Christmas had been a disaster. Just one long, dreary time of sadness and memories.

Things were even worse now. Instead of heading back to school after the Christmas and New Year holidays, Joshua had to look for a job. "We don't have much money, Josh," Mom had said. "We have to tighten our belts and find ways to get along. I've had to let poor Annie go, and now you'll need to pitch in and find work."

Joshua punched his pillow. Surely he would wake up from this nightmare and everything would be the way it used to be. But it was no dream.

"What about me?" Joshua said out loud, hating the guttural sound of his voice. His dad was gone. He'd been dismissed from the boys' choir because his voice changed. Now he couldn't go to school. The rugby team had a good chance of winning the pennant, too! What else could go wrong?

Joshua pushed his comforter away and sat up. He'd put off looking for a job all week. It was Friday. He'd *have* to go job hunting today.

The old gas lights had been sealed when the house was electrified ten years ago. Joshua tugged the long string attached to a bulb. The light glared in his eyes.

He looked out the window at the dismal day. The milkman had deposited bottles of milk and cream on their back stoop, and the horse pulling the carriage was clomping down the cobblestone alley. Next door, the neighbor had opened his carriage house and was cranking up his brand-new Model T Ford.

Joshua washed quietly in the bathroom. Then he tiptoed back to his room to dress—careful not to wake Mrs. Fryor, who snored loudly down the hall in the room that used to be his.

Pushing aside the knickers that hung neatly

in the closet, Joshua grabbed his blue suit and tossed it on the bed. He didn't want to go to work. He didn't know the first thing about job hunting.

But he had to go.

After dressing he brushed his blond hair with some pomade, then headed to the kitchen.

"Good morning, Josh," his mother greeted him. She put a pot of coffee on the gas stove, then looked her son up and down. "Good! You're wearing your best suit. It makes you look older."

"Do you think I can go back to school someday?" Joshua asked.

Mom turned her attention to a pot of bubbling oatmeal. "I'm sorry. I can't afford to send you back to the academy this year. Even public school is out of the question. We really need money, Josh. Your father made some poor investments, and . . . well, you don't need to worry about all the details. Once things settle down and we get all the rooms rented, maybe . . ." She turned a switch on the stove, and the burner flame went out with a loud *POP!* "Maybe I'll even get the electric stove I've always wanted."

Joshua recalled what Mr. Williams, the family lawyer, had told them right after Dad's death. His father had left only a small insurance policy and an even smaller bank account, along with large, outstanding debts.

"You finished eighth grade early, and with high marks, too," Mom continued. "Your father had great hopes for you, Joshua." She looked sad as she spooned oatmeal into a bowl and sprinkled brown sugar over it. "It will be hard to find decent work now that the war is over. You're only thirteen, and I don't want you working in a sweat shop."

"I'm going to Dad's bank to see if they need a messenger."

"No!" Mom said quickly. "Not there! Can't you try another bank? Or perhaps a department store? C. Crawford Hollidge is a nice store. Of course I wouldn't want anyone to see you there, but if you could work in the office . . ."

"You don't want anyone to know I'm working, do you." It wasn't a question.

"It will be better that way. After all, we have our pride. Perhaps you could find work with one of the music publishers. They would probably remember you from the Boston Boys' Choir."

"No!" Joshua snapped. "I told you I'm finished with music."

Mom shook her head and pulled the pot onto the side of the stove. "Don't eat any more of this oatmeal, Joshua. Aunt Caroline always has a big breakfast."

"Mrs. Fryor is *not* my aunt," Joshua grumbled.

Mom sat at the table. "I told you, our neighbors would never tolerate a rooming house on their street. I don't want them to know we have a paying boarder. So, she is now your Aunt Caroline."

"She's so cranky and mean. It's no wonder her family put her out."

"Hush! It's a shame when someone gets old, to think their family doesn't want them," Mom whispered. "Besides, they didn't put her out. They're paying a nice monthly fee for us to keep her here."

"She's got *my* bedroom," Joshua reminded her. He opened a bottle of cream and drizzled it on his oatmeal.

"Things have to be different now." Mom touched his shoulder. "Be careful where you go today. Stay away from the tenements. And please don't go to your father's bank."

When Joshua finished his oatmeal, he pulled

on his bulky overcoat. Mom handed him some coins. "Take the El, Josh. Remember, you don't want just *any* job." She kissed him on the forehead. "I'll worry if you're not back before dark."

Joshua had only taken the elevated train twice by himself and then he went directly to State Street to Dad's bank. He felt queasy. Mom was treating him as if he were suddenly all grown up—like she was expecting him to find work and take Dad's place or something. It wasn't fair!

Joshua headed out the front door. Nightshade Lane was awake now. A couple of automobiles rattled down the street, steering around a horse and carriage. Joshua remembered how excited and proud they were when Dad bought their new Peerless automobile. But the first thing Mom did after Dad died, was to sell it to Mr. Williams. Since then, when it was too far to walk, they had to take a cab or the El.

They lived in a nice neighborhood not far from downtown Boston, on a street of brick-front houses with bay windows and wrought-iron gates. How long would they be able to live here? Joshua wondered as he headed toward the elevated station on the next block. And where on earth would he ever find work?

Joshua paid his fare and found a seat next to the window. Well-dressed patrons got on at his stop, but he noticed poorer people coming aboard as the train continued into town. There were men in overalls and women in faded coats. Even children, carrying lunch pails, were on their way to work. Joshua almost asked one boy where he was employed, thinking there might be a job for him in the same place. The boy's eyes seemed far away, though, and Joshua changed his mind remembering what his father had told him: "Don't talk to strangers in town. Some of them are from different worlds, Josh."

Several passengers wore gauze masks. The influenza epidemic had everyone afraid. Joshua turned his face to the window—away from the man who was coughing next to him. Even though Joshua had already had the flu, he wasn't taking any chances.

The sun was shining brightly and streaming through the grimy windows. The train stopped again, and the sweet aroma of chocolate from the nearby candy factory drifted into the car. The slender, gray Custom House Tower piercing the skyline caught Joshua's attention.

Dad never did get to take him to the top of the tower like they had planned. Dad said the city was beautiful from up there, but Josh would never see it now.

The warmth and the constant rattle of the train made Joshua sleepy. He closed his eyes.

His thoughts drifted back to Dad's funeral.

*The sweet smell of flowers and fresh earth of the new graves permeated the cemetery. There were many other families weeping over new graves, too. Thousands had perished in the influenza outbreak.*

*Mom asked, "Josh, won't you sing one hymn for us? 'A Prayer to the Good Shepherd' was your father's favorite."*

*"No!" Joshua's voice rang out over the soft murmurs of relatives and friends. "Don't ask me to sing. I can't. Not at Dad's funeral!"*

"Hey, boy!" Someone shook Joshua's arm. The man in the next seat. "Wake up."

Joshua awoke with a start. "Where are we?" he asked.

"This is Atlantic Avenue."

Joshua had missed his stop. He got off the El

and looked around, bewildered. The icy air smelled of sea and fish. Where was he? He blocked his eyes from the sun and saw the Custom House Tower. State Street must be nearby.

Horses and carriages crowded the streets. The blaring honks of automobile horns added to the commotion. On the opposite sidewalk a man with a brightly colored wheelbarrow called out, "Fresh haddock and halibut!"

A newsboy, who looked to be about sixteen, darted around the traffic, hollering out the headlines. His brown woolen knickers were held up by bright red suspenders. Plaid shirttails hung below his open jacket. Strands of unruly carrot-colored hair had slipped out from under his soft gray cap. Joshua watched the boy in awe as he wove in and out between the cars and the carriages, yelling in a high-pitched voice, "Extra! Robbery in Revere." He'd stop at each vehicle, slide the latest copy of the newspaper into the driver's window, and grab the coins with the same hand.

Suddenly the traffic unsnarled and started moving again. The newsboy hopped onto the sidewalk, bumping into Joshua.

"Hey, you! Watch where you're going!" the boy exclaimed, scowling at Joshua. "Get outta my way."

Joshua struggled to retain his balance. "You bumped into *me!*"

The newsboy stepped closer. "Don't argue with me, pip-squeak."

"I wasn't arguing," Joshua snapped. "Get away from me."

At this moment two more boys, who also carried newspaper bags over their shoulders, appeared. One—a tall, skinny fellow—shook his finger at Joshua. "Don't you know you're askin' for trouble?" he warned. "This is Charlestown Charlie himself!"

"Did you hear what Shawn said?" The red-headed newsboy put his face close to Joshua's—so close, Joshua could almost count the freckles that dotted his nose. "Everyone in Boston—except you—knows it don't pay to argue with *me.*" And Charlestown Charlie gave Joshua a shove that knocked him to the ground.

# CHARLESTOWN CHARLIE

THE SHARPNESS OF THE CEMENT CUT THROUGH Joshua's trousers, and he felt a warm trickle of blood on his knee.

Charlestown Charlie bent over Joshua, who rubbed his gashed leg. "What's the matter, kid?" Charlie snickered. "Are you hurt? Are you gonna cry?"

The third boy, who seemed younger—about Joshua's age—watched with dark, solemn eyes. "Leave him alone, Charlie." The boy's voice was soft, with a slight accent. Joshua realized suddenly that this was not a boy at all—it was a girl in boy's clothing!

"I got off the El at the wrong station," Joshua explained, looking up at Charlie. "All I want is to get back to State Street."

Surprisingly, Charlestown Charlie put out his hand. "Get up, kid."

Joshua hesitated, then took Charlie's hand and was lifted almost off his feet. "Thanks," he muttered, brushing snow and dirt off his torn trousers.

"So you want to go to State Street. What are you going to do there, rob a bank?" Charlie demanded.

"No, I was looking for a job," Joshua answered. "But now my pants . . ."

"Oh, his pants are torn!" said the boy called Shawn with a wink at the others. "What a cryin' shame."

Charlie unhitched the newspaper bag from his shoulders and set it on the sidewalk. "What kind of job is up on State Street?"

"I . . . I don't know. A messenger, I guess."

"Why don't you sell papes like us?" Charlie asked.

"Papes? You mean newspapers? How would I sell newspapers?"

"You saw me, didn't you? Do what I do. Go where the people are—in the street, or at the shops, or the train stations. Yell out the most exciting news of the day and they'll buy your papes."

"I don't think I can do that," Joshua said.

Charlie reached into his bag. "I've got one more pape in here," he said, shoving it at Joshua. "Get out there and sell it."

"Yeah, this is your job interview," Shawn said with a laugh. "Let's see you do your stuff."

"I don't want to sell papers." Joshua thrust the paper back at Charlie.

"Why not? Ain't sellin' newspapers good enough for ya?" Charlie came closer. "You're probably not smart enough. You're just a stuck-up snob."

The dark-eyed girl spoke again. "Maybe he's not the type to sell papers. Maybe he's from Back Bay somewhere."

"That's right, Angel. He ain't got what it takes," said Shawn. "Highfalutin snob from Back Bay."

"I can do anything you can do," Joshua blurted angrily. He grabbed the paper from Charlie and read the headlines: "Bank Robbery in Revere. Relative of mayor suspected of embezzling." Charlie hawked the headline "Robbery in Revere," but Joshua didn't think that was the biggest news. There were lots of robberies in Revere. But this was a *bank* robbery. And the mayor's relative was under suspicion.

A shiny Peerless town car was stopped in the street, waiting for two horse-drawn carriages to go by. Joshua ran up to the driver's window. "Good morning, sir," he said loudly through the glass. "I have the latest news. A robbery and scandal in Revere." The well-dressed driver opened the window. Joshua continued. "A bank was robbed, and it looks like the mayor himself may be involved."

"Really? The mayor?" the driver asked. "Give me that paper. I own property in Revere."

"Here you are, sir." Joshua thought about the plot of land his father had purchased in Revere a year ago—land that was now up for sale. "I share your concerns," he said. "We own property out there, too."

The driver hesitated for a moment, then his face broadened into a grin. "You share my concerns?" He burst out laughing. "You own property in Revere . . ." He glanced down at Joshua's torn pants and chuckled some more. "You're full of baloney!" He pulled out two coins. "Here's a nickel for the paper, and keep the quarter for yourself. You gave me the best laugh I've had in a long time."

"Thank you, sir," said Joshua. "I appreciate your generosity."

"A gentleman, too! You'll do well in business." The driver closed the window and drove off, still chuckling.

"Here's the nickel for your paper," said Joshua, flipping it to Charlie. "The price of the paper is only three cents. So you made two cents' profit." He folded his arms. "But I keep the quarter tip."

"*A quarter tip!*" Angel said in amazement.

Charlie frowned. Joshua wondered if he would start pummeling him again. But instead he shrugged and pocketed the coin. "So you sold one paper. What's your name, kid?"

"Joshua Harper."

"Joshua Harper," Charlie mimicked in a high voice. "Such a fancy name!" He turned to his companions. "And did you hear what the man called him? A *gentleman*, no less. What do you think, fellers? Should we give Gentleman Josh a try?"

*Gentleman Josh?*

Charlie crossed his arms, thinking. "Tell you what. You can work for me like Shawn and Angel, here. I buy the papes, and you sell them for me. I'll pay you a penny apiece."

"A penny a paper? I'd have to sell a hundred papers a day to make a dollar."

"That's my offer. Take it or leave it."

"I'll leave it." Joshua started to walk away, then stopped. "Where do you buy your papers? Why can't I buy them directly from the company?"

Shawn and Angel gasped. Charlie's eyes narrowed. "Listen, pip-squeak, I was doin' you a favor offerin' you a job."

Shawn gave Joshua a warning glare. "Charlestown Charlie sells the *Boston Traveler* for this whole district," he said.

"How can one person handle the whole district?" Joshua asked.

"I have my own newsboys," Charlie answered. He pushed Shawn aside and grabbed Joshua by the collar of his coat. "So now you're thinkin' you'll take over and compete with me?"

"No, I wouldn't do that," Joshua said cautiously. "I told you I don't know anything about selling newspapers. Let me go."

Charlie let go of Joshua's collar with a shove. "Do you want the job or not?"

"Where would I work?"

"I'd try you out on the corner of State and Devonshire—where the snobs are. They'd like Gentleman Josh. You'll need to show up here every mornin' at six o'clock to pick up your papes. This is where I get my papers dropped off. We meet at two to divvy up the kale." Charlie saw Joshua's confused look. "Kale—that's *money*. Get it? Then you pick up the evenin' edition and you sell those until seven o'clock and you come here again with the kale."

"Six o'clock until seven? That's a long day."

"Ain't that too bad!" said Shawn.

"Look," Charlie explained. "I got plenty of young kids wantin' to work for me. I buy the papes and you guys work for *me*."

Joshua thought about the newsboys he'd seen in the past. Did they all work for Charlie?

"Listen, kid. I'm doin' you a favor. Be here bright and early on Monday mornin'. Okay?"

"I'll think about it," Joshua said. "If I decide to do it I'll be here at six on Monday."

"You can make at least a buck a day if you work hard," Charlie said. "Could you make that much as a messenger?"

"Maybe."

"I take care of everything—the papers, the route. All you have to do is bring a cart. You'll need it to carry the papers from here to State Street."

"How am I supposed to bring a cart on the El every day?" Joshua asked. "I thought you took care of *everything*." Shawn nudged Angel, and Joshua wondered if he'd gone too far.

Charlie stuck his face close to Joshua's. "I'm tellin' you—again—be careful how you talk to Charlestown Charlie. It could be dangerous, *Gentleman Josh*." He stood back, crossed his arms, then nodded. "Okay, I'll provide the cart." He shot a warning glance at Shawn and Angel. "Just so you know, the only reason I'm doin' this is that I need someone up on State Street. Gentleman Josh might be just the ticket." He turned again to Joshua. "Monday mornin' at six." Then Charlestown Charlie signaled his friends, and the three walked away toward the wharves.

Joshua sighed. He couldn't go looking for any other job with torn trousers, so he might as well go home. He found the El station at the corner, followed the signs that said NORTHBOUND, then waited for the train. He supposed a dollar a day wasn't so bad. At least until he found another job. And maybe he'd get tips like he did today.

He couldn't tell Mom. She'd die if she found out Josh was peddling newspapers on State Street.

# JOSHUA'S SECRET

WHEN JOSHUA GOT HOME, HIS MOTHER WAS IN THE parlor talking to a tall, well-dressed man who had his back to Joshua. He took the front stairs two at a time and raced down the hallway to his room.

At that moment Mrs. Fryor came out of the bathroom, leaning on her cane. "Watch out!" she shrieked. "This is no place to be running."

"I'm sorry, Mrs. Fryor . . . Aunt Caroline. I was just . . ."

"No excuses!" She hobbled back toward her bedroom, then stopped. "What happened to you?" she asked, looking down at Joshua's trousers.

"I . . . fell," he answered.

"You should be more careful. That's a nice suit."

"It wasn't my fault."

"Humph!" Aunt Caroline snorted. "Were you in a fight?"

Joshua could feel his face reddening. "Um, not exactly."

"Well, what *exactly?*" Aunt Caroline leaned on her cane and waited.

Joshua tried to avoid the woman's eyes. This was none of her business!

"A fellow knocked me down." There. That was all she'd get for an answer. He tried to pass her, but Aunt Caroline held up her cane, blocking the way.

"Your mother will be upset if she sees those pants."

"I know," said Joshua impatiently. "That's why I've got to change my clothes."

"After you change, bring your trousers into my room. I'll see what I can do to fix them."

"Could you?"

She bent over with difficulty and examined the tears. "Hm, maybe I can take a piece from the cuff and do some patching." She stood up and tapped Joshua lightly with the cane. "Go on, now. Get changed. Then bring those trousers to me straight away."

Joshua nodded and headed quickly to his

room. "Thanks, Mrs. Fryor—er—Aunt Caroline," he called before closing the door.

After changing into comfortable knickers, Joshua took his trousers to Aunt Caroline's room. "I've brought my pants," he said softly as he entered. "I hope you can fix them, if it's not too much trouble. I didn't want my mother to know. She's worried about money and—"

"Well, don't think for one minute I'm going to keep secrets from your mother," the old lady stated emphatically. "I'm only trying to fix them so they won't look so bad." She turned the trousers inside out. "I used to repair my children's clothing. We had plenty of money, but I never believed in being wasteful. Waste not, want not."

She sat by the window. The sunlight seemed to shine right through her skin, and her snow-white hair glowed like an angel's. Only, Aunt Caroline was no angel. Aunt Caroline was wrinkled, crotchety, and bossy. But at least she offered to fix his pants, and Joshua was grateful for that.

"All right, Joshua," said Aunt Caroline. "Tell me what's going on."

"It's no one's business."

"Now that I'm going to mend your pants, I'm

in on your secret. I don't want to be part of something that could be dishonest, or dangerous."

Dangerous? Dishonest? He had to tell Aunt Caroline the truth. "Please don't tell my mother," he begged as he slumped onto the window seat. "I'm going to sell newspapers."

Joshua told Aunt Caroline about his encounter with Charlestown Charlie, and how he successfully sold one paper and got a nice tip.

"Charlie says he'll take care of everything. At first I didn't think I'd want to sell papers, but Charlie talked me into it. He thinks people will like me. He says I'd be good up on State Street, where the snobs are—because he says *I'm* a snob—just because I'm polite," Joshua concluded.

"People on State Street knew your father," said Aunt Caroline. "And many of them went to the concerts where you used to sing. Someone will be sure to recognize you. Your mother will be horrified when she finds out."

"You're not going to tell her, are you?"

"No. But you'll need to tell her yourself before she hears it from someone else."

There was a knock on the door. "Aunt Caroline?" It was Mom.

"Just a minute, Gwendolyn." Aunt Caroline quickly tucked the trousers under the chair cushions. "Come in!"

"I wanted to let you know we have a new boarder. His name is Marc Muggeridge. He's a respectable gentleman—intelligent, educated. I think you'll like him." She looked at Joshua as if seeing him for the first time. "Oh, Joshua. How nice that you're visiting with Aunt Caroline. Did you find a job?"

Joshua nodded nervously. "Um . . . maybe."

"Oh, just *maybe?* Did you go to any of the other banks?"

"I may have a job . . . um . . . for a newspaper. I'll find out on Monday."

"That's wonderful. What newspaper?"

Joshua frowned. What papers did Charlie sell? "The *Boston Traveler.*"

"What a coincidence!" Mom exclaimed. "Mr. Muggeridge is an editor for the *Traveler.* Maybe you can go to work with him."

"I have to be at work at six o'clock on Monday morning."

"It's not even daylight then," Mom exclaimed. "You can't go into town at that hour."

"I have to. My boss told me so. And I won't be home until after seven o'clock at night."

"Those are terrible hours, Joshua."

"It's only for a while. Just to see how it works out."

"Isn't there something about child labor laws that would prohibit those hours?" Aunt Caroline asked.

"Nobody pays any attention to those laws." Mom sighed. "Well, we *do* need the money. Try it for now, until we get ahead a little financially. Having Mr. Muggeridge here will help with the bills. Maybe he can do something about those hours they want you to work."

Joshua and Aunt Caroline exchanged glances.

"I'm sure you don't want Mr. Muggeridge to feel any obligation to your family," Aunt Caroline said in a scolding tone to his mother. "After all, Gwendolyn, this is a business arrangement you have with your new boarder."

Mom looked embarrassed. "Oh...of course. That's right. We shouldn't ask favors of Mr. Muggeridge. At least not right away. But I simply *must* tell him that Joshua is working in the same company."

"I'll be working all over the place, Mom. I'll probably never even see Mr. Mugg . . . whatever his name is," Joshua stammered.

His mother smiled. She'll tell him, Joshua thought. I know her. She'll try to get me a better job or something. And then I'll have to tell her the truth.

"What will you be doing for the *Traveler?*" Mom inquired. "And how much do they pay?"

Joshua hesitated, then answered, "I'll be helping with . . . distribution."

"Distribution. My goodness. That sounds important. How much do they pay?" she asked again.

"It depends on . . . how many papers are distributed. I should do all right."

Mom looked puzzled, then shrugged. "Well, Mr. Muggeridge will be moving in next week, so that will give us some money on a *steady* basis. You can help me get his room ready this weekend, Joshua." Mom turned and left, leaving the door open.

"Thank you," Joshua whispered when Mom was out of hearing.

"Let's get something clear, young man. As I said, I'm not about to help you keep secrets from your mother," Aunt Caroline declared. "She's bound to hear it from someone." Her voice softened. "But I don't see any need to bring it up right now."

Joshua nodded. What Aunt Caroline said was true. If he worked for Charlie, Mom would find out sooner or later.

"You know, you don't *have* to show up on Monday," said Aunt Caroline. "You'd probably never see that Charlie fellow again."

Charlie had called Joshua a stuck-up snob. Shawn and Angel had said Joshua didn't have what it takes. Well, he'd show them. He'd sell one hundred papers on Monday, and *then* he'd quit.

When Charlie sees how many papers I sell, Joshua thought, he'll beg me to stay on. And maybe I will or maybe I won't.

"I'll show up," Joshua told Aunt Caroline. "It's something I've got to do—even if it's just for one day."

# GENTLEMAN JOSH ON THE JOB

AT PRECISELY SIX O'CLOCK ON MONDAY MORNING Joshua stood on the corner near the El station where he had first met Charlie. Wind whistled around the buildings, and waves lapped briskly against the boats tied to the docks nearby. The harbor air was raw. Ice had formed on the edges of street puddles, and in the early morning sunlight Joshua could see his own breath. He stomped his feet to keep warm, glad to be wearing his heavy gray knickers and black woolen jacket. He pulled his cap down as far as he could, then sank his hands deep into his pockets. Where was Charlie?

"Well, if it ain't Gentleman Josh himself. All ready for work?" Charlie appeared from an alley, pulling a wooden cart. The sides had been built up with extra boards to keep the papers from falling out.

"I'm ready," Joshua answered.

"You've got enough papes here to keep you busy all morning. You better get up to State Street before the crowds come."

"How many papers are in there?" Joshua asked.

"About fifty."

"What if I run short? I want to sell a hundred."

"A hundred, eh?" Charlie laughed. "Don't worry. I'll come by and check on you. If you need more, I'll get them to you."

"What if someone needs change?"

"Didn't you bring any?"

Joshua pulled some nickels and pennies from his pocket. "I have some. But what if—"

"There you go again. 'What if!' Just get up there and sell papers." Charlie dragged a canvas bag from the wagon and tossed it to Joshua. BOSTON TRAVELER was stenciled on the cloth.

Joshua pulled his arm through the strap, then asked, "How do I get to State Street?"

Charlie yanked Joshua around by the shoulder. "Go up this street to the end." He pointed his finger and spoke slowly as if Joshua were a little kid. "Turn right and you're on State Street. Once you get there you can go up Devonshire, then down Milk Street, and around the whole shebang, as far as I'm concerned. Just stay around the banks and sell those papes." He gave Joshua a shove. "Hurry up and get goin'!"

Joshua took hold of the cart's handle. "One more thing. If I get tips, they're mine."

"Sure, kid. You'll sell these fifty papes for three cents a copy. Then you give me a dollar. That leaves you fifty cents plus tips. Hey, I'm letting you have the use of the wagon for nothin', so don't complain. That's one dollar for me. Right? If you can sell the other fifty later, you owe me another dollar and you'll have made a whole dollar today—plus tips that you get to keep for yourself."

Joshua added the sums quickly in his head. "I guess so." He hoped Charlie wasn't cheating him. The fifty-cent commission seemed like a lot of money.

"I'll see how you do today," Charlie said as he headed down the street. "Then I'll decide about keepin' you on."

And I'll decide about keeping *you* on! Joshua

thought as he took off up the sidewalk, pulling the load of papers.

At State Street he tucked his cart in a nearby alley, took out one paper, then sat on the back steps of an office building to read the front page. Most of the headlines were about the end of the war and people way off in France somewhere. But here was something local. The Strong-Last Shoe Company was moving to Lynn, Massachusetts. Two hundred workers in Boston would be out of jobs. Joshua thought about the factory workers he saw on the train and in the streets, carrying their lunch pails. What would happen to them? "More than half the discharged employees would be women," the newspaper story said.

**"STRONG-LAST SHOE COMPANY MOVES TO LYNN. HUNDREDS LOSE JOBS."** That was a catchy headline.

Joshua stuffed his shoulder bag with papers, then hid the cart under a stairway. Out on the street people were hurrying to work. "Extra!" Joshua called out. "Shoe company moves to Lynn."

Only one person took a paper. "Project!" the choir director, Mr. Albert, used to command Josh.

"Breathe from the diaphragm—let your voice float out on the wings of your breath."

But that was when Joshua was a boy soprano and had a voice. When his voice began to change, he croaked instead of sang. He wasn't singing today. He was hawking papers.

"STRONG-LAST SHOES MOVES TO LYNN," Joshua yelled, holding the paper up to show the headlines. "HUNDREDS OF WOMEN LOSE THEIR JOBS!"

A man stopped and took a copy, handing Joshua a dime. "That's bad news for Boston." He walked away, glancing over the front page without waiting for his change. Joshua shoved the dime into his pocket and pulled out another paper.

"BAD NEWS FOR BOSTON! STRONG-LAST SHOES MOVES TO LYNN. HUNDREDS LOSE THEIR JOBS!" Joshua's voice boomed and echoed across the street. People stopped and took his papers. Some folks who had passed him by turned and came back.

"Are they building a factory in Lynn?" one woman asked.

"I guess so, ma'am," Joshua answered. "Perhaps this will be good news for other towns."

"I may try to get a job out there," the lady said as she looked over the paper.

"Good luck, ma'am." Joshua nodded. "Lynn might be a nice place to work and live, I would think."

"Thank you." She smiled. "You're a ray of sunshine." She handed Joshua a nickel. "Keep the change."

"JOBS AVAILABLE AT SHOE FACTORY IN LYNN!" Joshua called out as he walked up the sidewalk.

A small crowd gathered to buy Joshua's papers.

"That should make real estate values go up in Lynn," a well-dressed man said to another.

"Boston's loss, Lynn's gain," agreed his companion.

"BOSTON'S LOSS, LYNN'S GAIN," Joshua yelled, handing out the papers as fast as he could. "POSSIBLE REAL ESTATE BOOM IN LYNN."

In a few minutes all the papers in his bag were sold and Joshua's jacket pocket jingled with change. He hurried to the alley, filled the bag, and returned to the street. "NEW JOBS AVAILABLE IN LYNN."

Suddenly Joshua recognized one of the officers from his father's bank having his shoes shined by a bootblack. Joshua pulled the visor of his cap down over his eyes.

The man hollered to him. "Hey, newsboy! Give me a paper." He pulled his foot off the bootblack's stand and yanked some change out of his pocket. The bootblack, who seemed about Joshua's age, looked up impatiently. The man put his foot back on the stand, and the boy began buffing the shoe with a soft brush.

The banker handed Joshua the correct change. "Are you new here on the street?"

"Um, yes, sir. I'm new here."

"You look familiar."

Joshua didn't answer. He looked up and was relieved to see the man was reading the headlines while the shoeshine boy put paste on his other shoe.

He didn't even give me a tip, the cheapskate.

"EXTRA, EXTRA! SHOE COMPANY CLOSES IN BOSTON."

Within an hour, Joshua had sold all the papers

in his cart and headed back to Atlantic Avenue to meet Charlie. He raced down the sidewalk towing the cart by its handle, careful to avoid pedestrians who might be potential customers. "Excuse me, ma'am," he called. "Excuse me, sir."

The corner at Atlantic Avenue was empty. Joshua saw Angel coming toward him. She was wearing boys' tweed knickers with long black socks. Her newspaper bag hung over the shoulder of her black woolen jacket. A little girl of about three or four clung to her hand. The two girls both wore gray knit caps pulled over their ears. Curly raven-black hair peeked out in wisps around their faces.

"Where's Charlie?" Angel asked.

"I don't know. I ran out of papers," Joshua answered. "I hope he's not looking for me."

"You can take mine," Angel said. "My mama is sick. I tried to work and watch Maria, too, but I can't do it. I've got to take Maria home." Maria buried her face in Angel's leg.

"Is it the flu?"

"Yes. Maria and I had it last summer. I thought we would both die," Angel said. "My father went to Rhode Island to look for work, but then he got sick and stayed there. When Mama got the influenza, Auntie Flora, who lives downstairs, took care of Maria while I worked. But now Flora is sick. So I have to take care of Maria and work, too. But I can't do it, Joshua."

"Better take her home right away," Joshua said. "Your mother probably needs you."

Angel nodded and reached into her pocket. "I only sold a dozen papers. I hope Charlie ain't mad." She handed Joshua the money. "Can I trust you to give this to him?"

"Of course you can trust me," Joshua answered abruptly. "I wouldn't steal your money."

"I'm sorry, Joshua. It's just . . ." Angel's eyes filled with tears, and he looked away.

Maria began to whimper and reached up her hands to her sister. "Carry me, Angelina."

"My family calls me Angelina. That's my real name," Angel said with a half-smile. She picked up her sister. "I know you're tired," she whispered, "but I can't carry you the whole way. You're too heavy."

"Take the cart," Joshua offered. "Take her home in the cart."

Angel brightened. "Oh, thanks. That's a good

idea." She lowered her sister into the cart, took hold of the handle, and headed north. "Tell Charlie I'll bring the cart back later."

Joshua sat on the curbstone. He wondered about Angel. Why did she dress like a boy? Maybe she didn't have enough money to buy clothes.

Joshua counted the money in his own pocket. Almost three dollars. Not bad for an hour's work. Of course, he had to pay Charlie half of it. Still, he had another fifty papers to go. If he could make five dollars today, he'd have enough money for Mom to fill up the coal bin in the cellar. He put Angel's money in his pants' pocket. Angel had given him a couple of dozen more papers. He'd sell those in no time.

He was heading back to State Street when he spotted Charlie talking to a well-dressed middle-aged man with a mustache. Charlie had his hands on his hips and he looked mad.

"Hey, kid!" Charlie yelled when he caught sight of Joshua.

When Joshua reached them, Charlie said, "I've been hearin' you did *really* great up there on State Street. The big shots love you."

"I came back for more papers, but I met Angel and—"

"Hey, I'm talkin' to you. This here gentleman works for the newspaper. He wanted to meet you." Charlie turned to the man. "This here is Gentleman Josh."

The stranger spoke up. "I had an appointment up at the bank this morning and I saw you selling those papers like crazy. You sang out that headline like I've never heard it done before. You've got talent, kid. I think I could do business with someone like you."

Charlie rolled his eyes. "He's only been on the job one mornin'. Besides, he had a good headline to hawk."

"Now, Charlie," said the man, "I give you good tips for what you do, but you can't be everywhere at once. This young man seems to fit in up there in the banking district, and I think he can help me in that area."

"Selling papers?" Joshua was puzzled.

"Sure, you can still sell papers for Charlie. But I have some other work you can do for me on the side to make some extra money."

Charlestown Charlie looked daggers at Joshua and sputtered, "He's green. He don't know nothin'."

The man ignored Charlie and put out his hand. "So you're called Gentleman Josh?" He grinned. "It's nice to meet you, Josh. My name is Muggeridge. Marc Muggeridge."

Mom's new boarder!

# THE MYSTERIOUS
# MR. MUGGERIDGE

"HOW DO YOU DO?" JOSHUA STAMMERED, SHAKING the man's hand.

"Let me explain what we're talking about," Mr. Muggeridge said. "You see, I need someone like Charlie here who knows the ropes. So we've made a little business arrangement that's working out right well. Someday Charlie is going to be a reporter, aren't you, Charlie?" He slung his arm around Charlie, who gave Marc a smug grin. "He knows the business. And he knows what makes news," Mr. Muggeridge continued. "He keeps his eyes and ears open, and then reports anything newsworthy to me. I check it out, write it up, and I give Charlie some extra money for his help. You might say he's my apprentice."

"He's going to write for the *Boston Traveler*

someday?" Joshua asked. He couldn't picture Charlie writing anything, let alone a newspaper column.

"Whatsa matter, kid? You got a problem with that?" Charlie growled.

"Cut it out, Charlie!" Mr. Muggeridge admonished. "Charlie's learning the business, Josh, and being paid for it at the same time. I think you'd do well at this, too, from the way you handled yourself on State Street this morning."

"He had a good headline. *That's* why he sold so many papers," Charlie said with a frown.

"Gentleman Josh is creative with *his* headlines. He comes up with good lines that hook customers," Mr. Muggeridge said. "If he's in the banking area, he might hear of some leads for newspaper stories. If so, I'll make it worth his while. Two or three bucks a week for a lead—even more for a scoop—that could add up. What do you say, Josh?" He put out his hand again. "Do we have a deal?"

Joshua wasn't at all sure what this was about, but he shook Mr. Muggeridge's hand, anyway. "So you're a reporter?" he asked.

"Yes, I'm a reporter—and an editor. I was with the New York *World* down in New York City, but moved up here a month ago. Just now settling in." He clapped Charlie's shoulder. "When I met Charlie here I knew he'd be a great resource for me, and he's already come through with flying colors. I feel the same way about you."

Charlie interrupted. "I'm not sure I want Joshua sellin' my papes. He's cuttin' in on me already."

"Oh, don't get in a lather, Charlie," Mr. Muggeridge said. "You've got a great newsie here. You'd be foolish to let him go. The business I have with you and Joshua is altogether separate, so don't give him a hard time."

"I . . . I don't want to horn in on Charlie," Joshua said. "I'm not even sure what it is you want me to do, Mr. Muggeridge."

"Just keep your ears open for *anything interesting.* The war overseas made the big headlines, but now that the fighting is over, I'd like to zero in on news around Boston. If you hear about a robbery, or a fire, or some other disaster, let me know as soon as you can. Contact me—no one else. I'll take care of everything. If it turns into a scoop for me, you'll be paid for the tip." He scribbled on a slip of paper. "Here's my telephone number at the office and my business address. That's all you have to do, Josh. I'm sure you're the right person to be discreet when you search for news that might interest me."

"Discreet?" Charlie asked.

"Tactful. Diplomatic," Mr. Muggeridge explained. "I know I can count on Gentleman Josh being tactful and polite, but I'm not so sure about you, Charlie!" The reporter laughed and winked. But as he turned to leave he shot a warning look at Charlie. "Leave Josh alone, *Charles*. He won't cause any problems for you."

"Well, Mr. Mugg sure is keen on you," Charlie said icily after the reporter had left. "Let's get somethin' clear, pip-squeak. You don't cut in on *my* stories and *my* kale. If you do, you'll be in big trouble. Got it?"

"I get it, I get it," Joshua said. "I didn't go after this Mr. Mugg. I didn't try to butt in on you, Charlie."

The older boy nodded. "Okay. Keep your mouth shut about our arrangement with Mr. Mugg.

People don't talk when they know a reporter might be listenin'.'"

"I'll keep quiet."

Charlie looked around. "What did you do with the cart I lent you?"

"Angel has it. I let her take her little sister home in it."

"You *what?* Who said you could do that?"

"Her mother is sick, so Angel can't work. Angel tried to sell papers and watch her sister, too. But she couldn't, so she had to go home. I gave her the cart to carry Maria back."

"Whadda ya think I'm runnin' here? A taxi service?"

Joshua ignored Charlie's snide remark. "Here's the money that Angel collected for you and my money, too."

Charlie counted the money and stuffed it in his pocket. "Gentleman Josh to the rescue," he muttered.

"It was an emergency, Charlie!" Joshua's voice rose. "Some things are more important than *your* business."

Charlie looked mad enough to hit him, but

Joshua didn't flinch. The two boys stared at each other, their breath steaming in the cold air.

Then, surprisingly, Charlie changed the subject. "Okay, we'll get the cart later. There's another fifty papes waitin' for you. What are you gonna do with them?"

"I'll carry them up to State Street myself."

"Come get 'em, then."

Joshua followed Charlie to a side street. Stacks of the morning *Traveler* were piled on the sidewalk, covered with canvas. Charlie stuffed twenty-five papers into Joshua's bag, then flipped it around his neck so it hung down his back. He stacked the second batch into Joshua's arms. "Get up to State Street," he ordered. "And bring that cart to me when you come for the afternoon papes."

Joshua didn't answer. He shifted the bulk in his arms and headed for State Street.

Later, while Joshua was working on his corner, Angel returned with the cart.

"Thanks, Josh. I left Maria with my neighbor, Mrs. Clougherty. I told her I'd come right back."

"How's your mother?" Joshua stacked his armful of papers into the cart.

"She's weak. She coughed all night." Angel counted some coins in her hand. "I've got to get some fruit for her."

Across the street a vendor was selling apples and penny toys. "I'll get them. Wait here and watch my papers." Joshua darted to the opposite sidewalk. He bought six McIntosh apples for a nickel. Then he caught sight of a small celluloid doll among the penny toys. It wore a lace bonnet and pink crocheted dress.

"How much for the doll?" Joshua asked.

"A nickel."

"I thought these were *penny* toys." Joshua started to walk away.

"All right, kid, you can have it for three cents," the vendor called after him.

Joshua doled out the money, stuffed the doll in the apple bag, and ran back across the street. "Here, take these apples," he said. "Eat one yourself, Angel."

Angel took the package. "How much?"

"Nothing. Just take them. Oh"—he pulled out the doll—"give this to Maria."

Angel held the doll as if it was a treasure. "Oh Josh, you ain't gotta do that," she whispered. Then she wheeled around and raced down the side-walk.

Joshua was about to set up his newspapers again, when he noticed a group of poorly dressed girls skipping rope near the corner.

One child jumped into the swinging rope as the others chanted:

> "There was a little bird;
>
> Its name was Enza.
>
> I opened up the window,
>
> And in flew Enza."

Influenza had killed thousands of people, including his own dad! It wasn't a game. It wasn't something to sing about!

"Get away from here!" Joshua hollered at them.

The girls stopped jumping. One girl put her hands on her hips and stuck out her tongue.

"Get away from here yourself," she yelled.

"This is *my* corner," Joshua shouted. "Move away or I'll tell Charlestown Charlie."

Immediately the girls rolled up their jump rope and scurried away.

Charlie sure had a reputation around town.

Joshua held up the morning edition and projected his voice—just like Mr. Albert had taught him.

"*EXTRA!* STRONG-LAST SHOES MOVES TO LYNN!"

# THE NEW BOARDER

WHEN JOSHUA ARRIVED HOME THAT NIGHT, HIS mother was in the kitchen washing dishes.

"Thank goodness you're back," she said. "I was getting worried. I don't like the idea of you coming home so late, Josh."

"Well, I made over three dollars today." He emptied his pockets onto the kitchen table.

"Wonderful! Why do they pay you in change?"

"Money is money," Joshua answered.

"But all coins? Why didn't they give you paper currency?"

Joshua shrugged, avoiding her eyes. "What's for supper?"

"Red flannel hash. Your plate is on the pantry counter. It's cold now. You can warm it in the oven." She slipped the money into her apron pocket.

"I'm too hungry to warm it." Joshua brought the plate to the table and sat down. He noticed his mother had a larger stack of dishes than usual. "Did the new boarder move in today?"

"Yes, Mr. Muggeridge moved in lock, stock, and barrel. He has one of those newfangled type-writers upstairs. My beautiful old bedroom looks like an office."

Joshua stuffed a large spoonful of cold hash into his mouth. "Why didn't you keep your bed-room instead of moving into the den? At least you'd have a bed instead of the couch."

"Don't talk with your mouth full," Mom said with a frown. "The den is all right for me. Besides, there are personal papers and things of Dad's in the den that I still have to go through—things a stranger shouldn't see."

"So, is Mr. Muggeridge nice?"

"He's all right. He's looking forward to meet-ing you. I told him that you worked for the news-paper, too."

Joshua hoped Mr. Mugg hadn't already made the connection between Gentleman Josh and Joshua Harper.

"Joshua, when you're finished, would you dry

these dishes? I feel as if I've been chained to this kitchen." His mother held her hands up to the overhead light. "Just look at my hands. They were always so beautiful. Now they're all red and chapped." She sighed. "I wish Annie were still with us. I've never had to work a day in my life, and look at me now."

"I've worked all day, too, Mom. Just leave the dishes to dry themselves."

"I'd like you to meet Mr. Muggeridge," she said, setting the dish towel on the sink. "I've explained that you'll be calling him *Uncle Marc*."

"Uncle Marc?" Joshua exclaimed. "Mom! People will find out he's not my uncle. I feel like I'm lying."

"It's all right, Joshua. Mr. Muggeridge is satisfied with this arrangement. After all, he's in one of the finest neighborhoods in Boston. He knows I'm a widow and having difficult times. He's not going to let on to anyone that he's boarding here." She put the milk and butter in the icebox. "Go on and meet him. He's in the parlor."

Joshua wolfed down the rest of his dinner, then dropped the plate in the dishpan. "I'm going to bed. I'm too tired to meet anyone."

"But . . . I told him . . ."

Joshua raced noisily up the stairs and headed for his room.

Aunt Caroline's door was open; the light was on. "Is that you, Joshua? Come in here." she called.

Joshua stepped into the room, closing the door behind him.

"How did you do today?" Aunt Caroline's hands were folded over a book in her lap.

"I did all right. I sold over a hundred papers." He leaned forward and whispered, "I met Mr. Muggeridge on the street."

"Oh, really? He didn't mention that to us."

"He doesn't know I'm *me*. He only knows me as"—Joshua rolled his eyes—"*Gentleman Josh*."

Aunt Caroline stifled a laugh.

"It's not funny!" Joshua exclaimed. "If Mr. Mugg . . . er . . . Muggeridge realizes I'm Gentleman Josh, he might tell Mom."

"How did you meet him?"

"Through Charlie. Mr. Muggeridge asked me to work for him on the side. He wants me to find news around town and tell him about it so he can write stories for the paper."

"Well, there's nothing wrong in that. You might make some extra money."

Joshua paced nervously. "Charlie finds stories for him, too. Charlie thinks I'm horning in on him. What if he finds out that Mr. Muggeridge lives here—and he's my *Uncle Marc!*"

"What are you going to do?"

"I'll stay away from Mr. Mugg. I'll leave early and come home late. I can't let him know that Joshua Harper and Gentleman Josh are the same person."

Aunt Caroline raised her eyebrows. "Joshua, I think Mr. Muggeridge already knows who you are."

"How could he? Did you tell him?"

"Of course not. But Mr. Mugg—as you call him—was in the parlor looking at the photographs on the table. There's a picture of you there, Joshua. He had it in his hand."

"Oh, no!" Joshua sank into a chair. "I forgot about those pictures. Did he say anything?"

"Not a word. But he sure was eyeing that photograph, let me tell."

"Then he knows who I am." Joshua stood up.

"I'll have to talk to him. I'll ask him not to tell Mom that I'm a newsboy."

"Secrets have a way of coming out."

"I know, but this secret would upset her too much."

Aunt Caroline nodded. "All right. Now, would you take a look at this?" She held up her book. "It's a music book—mostly hymns and old songs."

Joshua waited.

"I'd like you to have it, Joshua. I'd like you to sing for me sometime. Your mother said you have a beautiful voice."

Joshua headed for the door. "I don't sing anymore and I don't want your book!" He rushed into the hall.

And ran right into Marc Muggeridge!

# A WARNING

"WELL, IF IT ISN'T GENTLEMAN JOSH!" MR. MUGGERIDGE exclaimed. "Where are you racing off to?"

"I . . . er . . . I'm going to my room."

Mr. Muggeridge stepped aside and made a sweeping bow. "Go right ahead."

Joshua hesitated. "Mr. Muggeridge? Can I talk to you?"

"Sure." The reporter crossed his arms and waited.

"Not here. Can we talk in your room?"

"Sure. Come on in."

Joshua entered what had been his parents' bedroom. A typewriter sat on a desk by the window. Papers cluttered a table, and two oak file cabinets now occupied the place where Mom's vanity had been.

Mr. Muggeridge pulled a leather briefcase from a chair, set it on the floor, and motioned for Joshua to sit down. "What do you want to talk about?" He sat on the edge of the bed and stroked his mustache.

Joshua wiggled uncomfortably in his seat. "This morning . . . in town . . . I thought you might be our new boarder. Mom said something about a reporter moving in . . . but I didn't say anything 'cause . . . well, my mother doesn't know that I'm a newsboy. She wouldn't like it."

"Sure, Joshua, I understand. Your mother and father were among the social elite. What do they call them? Boston Brahmins?" Mr. Mugg grinned. "Your mother doesn't want her neighbors to know she's taking in boarders. So, I can understand why you want to keep your . . . occupation . . . a secret, too."

"I'm not ashamed of selling papers," Joshua said. "Jobs are hard to find now that the war's over."

Mr. Mugg's expression became serious. "Joshua, you could get a job most anywhere. You've got class, and your father knew people in high places. Don't you know that? But instead, here you are working for Charlestown Charlie."

"He said I was a snob and didn't have what it takes."

"So do you have to prove yourself to Charlie? Or to yourself?"

"Both, I guess."

"Let me tell you something about Charlie. He's from an Irish immigrant family and he has ten sisters and brothers. He's driven—impelled—to work hard. That's about all you've got in common with him, Josh. You're both trying to help out your families."

"Mr. Muggeridge, Charlie buys the papers and then gets lots of kids to sell them for him. Couldn't I buy the papers directly—like he does? Then I could make more profit."

"Sure you could. The newspaper would probably sell directly to you if you asked them to. You might get into a lot of trouble with Charlie if you try to cut in on his territory, though. He's got his boys working for him, and no one dares to leave."

"I asked Charlie outright why I couldn't go directly to the paper, and I thought he was going to knock me out."

"Oh, Charlie acts real tough when he's scared. Believe it or not, I think he's worried about you. He's concerned that you might actually compete with him and he'd lose out."

"Charlie never seems scared. But he sure is *scary.*"

"Here's something else to think about, Josh. Charlie's the top newsboy in Boston, you know. But that's only because he has all you kids working for him and he's getting the credit at the paper. There are scholarships available for newsboys. If you start selling directly, you might find yourself eligible for a scholarship. Charlie qualifies. He's just too busy supporting his family to take time off to go to school."

"How come you know so much about Charlie? You've only been in town a month."

"He and I had a long talk one day. I dealt with kids like him in New York."

"He doesn't like me very much," Joshua said.

"Think carefully before you decide to cross Charlie."

"I don't want to cross him. I just want to make some kale . . . money." Joshua was surprised to hear Charlie's term slip out of his own mouth.

"Good." Marc Muggeridge walked over to Joshua and shook his hand. "You can trust your old Uncle Marc," he said. "You can call me Marc, you know. Without the *uncle*, if you prefer. Don't worry, I won't let on to your mother that you're a newsie. That's what we call newsboys in New York City."

"Charlie calls himself a 'newsie.'"

"He's been around, Josh." Marc grinned. "You know, Charlie's the one who found out about the shoe factory closing in Boston. His brother worked there. I paid him two bucks for that tip."

"Two bucks! No wonder he's afraid I'm horning in."

"There's enough news in Boston to go around. Now, if there was an earthquake or fire like they had years ago, that would be *big* news."

"That would be *awful* news," Joshua retorted. "You sound like you want a disaster or something, just for the headlines."

Marc Muggeridge shrugged. "I'm a reporter, Joshua. I think like a reporter."

Joshua got up to leave. "I'll let you know when I hear anything *big*."

"The bigger the better." Marc held the door

open. "By the way, I saw your picture down on the piano. You were wearing a choir robe. Do you sing?"

"No," Joshua replied, "I don't."

"That's not the way I heard it," said Marc as he closed the door.

Joshua headed to his room, then stopped. Aunt Caroline. He had left her room in a huff. He should go back and apologize. He knocked gently on her door.

"Come in." Aunt Caroline was in the same chair, but the book was no longer in her lap. "It's getting late. What is it, Joshua?"

"I came back to say I'm sorry for being so rude."

"I accept your apology. Now, come in and close the door."

Joshua went inside, then waited.

"I'm sorry I asked you to sing for me sometime. I didn't realize it would upset you so much. I will not make that mistake again."

Joshua sat on the edge of Aunt Caroline's bed. "I miss singing. Just after Dad died, when my voice changed, I couldn't hit the high notes, and it kept cracking. Sometimes I sounded like a frog.

The other boys kidded me. I knew when I joined the choir that sometime my voice would change and I'd have to leave. But when Mr. Albert, the choir master told me it was over . . ."

"I understand, Joshua. You had a beautiful gift, and perhaps you feel it was snatched away from you. Maybe you'll sing again someday—when you're ready. Perhaps your beautiful voice has been replaced by one that's even more beautiful."

"My new voice is awful," Joshua muttered. "I'm glad Dad never heard it."

Aunt Caroline continued. "I love Irish ballads sung by a real Irish tenor. However, my favorite male voice is baritone. It's a nice range to listen to. Easy on the ears." She paused. "Music has always been part of my life, Joshua, As long as there is music inside me, I never feel totally alone."

Joshua felt a rush of sadness for Aunt Caroline. Her family had not come to see her since she had moved into the Harpers' home. He traced the colorful quilt patterns with his finger. "I was a soloist, you know."

"I know."

"My dad was so proud that I was the soloist for the Boston Boys' Choir. He used to brag to everyone about it."

"Your mother told me how the director once said your voice was like a bell—lilting and clear. 'The most beautiful voice in Boston,' he said."

Joshua stood up. "Not anymore."

"It's all right, Joshua. I won't mention it again."

"Thank you. Good night."

"Oh, Josh," Aunt Caroline said as he was about to leave. "I've repaired your trousers." She pulled the pants out from a knitting bag by her chair. "Here. Take them back to your room and hang them up."

Joshua looked them over. "I can't even see where they were ripped," he said in amazement.

"I've had a lot of practice repairing clothes. I had two boys, you know." She smiled. "Maybe you'll meet them. I'm sure they'll come to visit me soon."

"Thank you, Aunt Caroline," Joshua said as he headed for the door. Then, on a sudden impulse, he turned around and kissed the older woman on her cheek. "Thank you," he whispered.

"You're welcome." She scooted him out with her hand. "Now go put those trousers away."

Joshua bathed, put on his pajamas and bathrobe, then went downstairs. Mom was finishing up in the kitchen. "Sorry I didn't help with the dishes, Mom," he said.

"Thank you for the money," she said. "Now I can pay the milkman tomorrow. I left some change on the table. You'll need it to get to work."

"I met Mr. Muggeridge—Marc—upstairs. I visited him in his room for a while."

"Good. He seems nice, and the extra money he's paying for his room and board will be helpful. Maybe things will be all right after all." She kissed his forehead. "Go to bed now. You need your sleep."

Back in his own room, Joshua climbed into bed and thought about Aunt Caroline. He was glad he had gone back to her room to apologize. She wasn't mad, either. She understood how he felt—that so much had been taken away from him: his friends, his voice, his father.

He closed his eyes and saw his father's face— his dark eyes and crinkling smile—the way he used to laugh and rumple Joshua's hair. Josh had always pulled away when he did that. He would give anything to have his father do it one more time.

"Oh, Dad, I'm sorry I couldn't sing at your funeral, and now my voice is gone." Joshua rolled over and clutched his pillow. "I miss you so much!" he whispered.

# JOSHUA GETS
# A SCOOP!

THE NEXT MORNING, WHILE IT WAS STILL DARK, Joshua could hear the tap, tapping of Mr. Mugg's typewriter. Joshua left for town in the freezing dawn, before the reporter appeared for breakfast.

Just as he arrived at his usual pickup corner, a horse-drawn wagon, with the words BOSTON TRAVELER painted in black letters on the side, pulled up to the curb. Charlie and the wagon driver piled stacks of newspapers on the sidewalk. Charlie dropped off the handcart, then faced Joshua.

"From now on I'll leave your papes piled on the handcart in that alley," he said, pointing to the dark walkway behind an office stationery store. "The owner of this establishment knows me. He said it's okay to pick your papes up here every morning."

"Shall I still meet you here for the evening papers?"

"Yeah. If I get here first, you'll see your pile over there covered with canvas. If I don't see you, I'll find you at State Street to pick up the money you owe me." Charlie climbed back onto the wagon. "Get busy, Gentleman Josh," he sneered as he and the driver drove noisily up the cobblestone street.

Back at his corner, Joshua called out the headlines, and people crowded around to buy his papers. When the rush hour was over, Joshua sat on the curb to count his money.

"Want a shine?"

Joshua looked up to see a boy about his own age carrying a wooden chest. He recognized him as one of the bootblacks who polished shoes along the streets.

"Do I look like I need a shine?" Joshua asked, pointing to his old boots.

The kid sat down beside him. "What's your name?"

"Josh."

"I'm Billy Boot. That's not my real name, but I

like it better than McGillicuddy. That's way too long. Everyone knows Billy Boot." The boy took off his woolen cap and scratched his dark blond hair. "Do you work for Charlestown Charlie?"

"Yeah," Joshua answered.

"I used to. But now I'm doin' shoe shines."

"How come?"

"I got tired of him bossin' me around."

"Did Charlie give you a hard time?"

"Oh, yeah. It was easier to become a bootblack than to have Charlie out to get me."

"Where did you get the kit?" Joshua asked, nodding at the smooth-finished wooden container.

"My uncle made it for me." Billy Boot opened the cleverly constructed box. "See? All my polish and brushes are in here. This part opens so the customer can rest his foot on the black rubber pad. Pretty clever, eh?"

"That's a real pip," Joshua agreed. "Do you make much money doing bootblack?"

"Enough to help out at home. I'm thinkin' of joinin' the union. There's a union in New York City, you know, for paperboys and bootblacks. But the union has yet to work somethin' out for us younger kids, 'cause of the new child labor laws." Billy closed the chest carefully and brushed the top off with his sleeve. "But I don't need the union. I got a lot of good customers," he said. "They all like me around here where the big shots work. They trust me."

"What do you mean, they trust you? With what? Their shoes?"

"I mean they trust *me*. They talk about business and things to each other while they wait in line for me to shine their shoes. It's like I'm one of them. They know me and they trust me."

Maybe this Billy Boot knew things that Marc could use for the *Traveler*. "What kind of things do they talk about in front of you?"

"Well, things like who's been hired and fired and where they're investin' their money." Billy laughed. "If I had money, I'd know where to put it. Trouble is, I ain't got none." He sat back and grinned. "But I know a lot that's goin' on in Boston," Billy bragged.

"Oh, sure you do," Joshua said.

Billy bristled. "Just this mornin' I heard something *really* big."

"You're just full of talk," Joshua egged him on.

"You'll hear about it soon enough in the papers."

"If I'm going to hear about it in the papers, why can't you tell me?"

Billy Boot leaned close to Joshua. "One of the big shots at the Jupiter Bank has been fired. They found he'd been stealin' money. They're tryin' to keep it quiet, but—"

"I thought you said it would be in the papers," said Joshua.

"When they throw the banker in jail, everyone will know. They can't keep *that* quiet."

"I'll believe it when I see it in the paper," said Joshua. "You could be making it all up."

"I told you . . ." Billy hesitated and then said, "Okay. I'll tell you who it was that stole the money. Then you'll believe me when it all comes out in the news."

"Tell me, then."

"Don't let on to anyone where you heard it. Promise?"

"I promise," said Joshua.

Billy moved closer to Joshua and spoke in a low voice. "He's a highbrow around town, and at the bank, too. His name's Manderville."

"Okay," said Joshua. "I'll watch for it in the paper."

"Well, I gotta go now. We could freeze to death sittin' here," said Billy, standing up. He blew on his hands, then pulled on a pair of patched knitted mittens. "The early lunchers will be comin' out for a shine." He picked up his bootblack box and headed down the street.

"See you later, Billy," Joshua called.

Joshua didn't waste time getting to the *Traveler* offices. On the face of the tall, gray building in the center of the square, the words THE BOSTON TRAVELER were inscribed in large black letters. Inside he pulled off his hat and asked a receptionist the way to Marc Muggeridge's office. He took the elevator to the second floor and through the open grating he could see lots of people rushing around—just like in the flickers—the new movie shows.

The second floor was a large, open room filled with desks and private offices around the perimeter. Joshua found Marc's office and knocked.

"Come in!"

Joshua burst into the office. "I've got a scoop for you," he said breathlessly.

Marc listened to Joshua's story. "Where did you hear this information?" he asked.

Joshua hesitated. "I don't want to tell. I might get the kid in trouble."

"Is he a reliable source?"

"Yes. He swears it's the truth."

Marc whistled softly. "Manderville. One of the big Boston names caught up in a scandal. This *is* a scoop, Joshua. Don't tell anyone else, okay?"

"Okay."

Marc wrote something on a piece of paper, then stood up. "If this is as big as I think, you'll be compensated well."

"What if Charlie comes to you with the same story?"

"You came first. That's it, as far as I'm concerned." Marc gave Joshua an understanding smile. "I don't have to tell Charlie where I found out. So don't you worry."

Joshua sighed. "Thanks, Marc. See you tonight."

Charlie was waiting for Joshua when he went to collect the evening edition. "I saw you today at the *Traveler* office. What were you doin' there?"

"I had to see someone . . ."

"Yeah, right. You had to see Mr. Mugg."

"Why do you say that?"

"Why else would you be there?"

Joshua took a deep breath. "Look, Charlie, Marc told you that he was going to use me for scoops, too. So naturally, if I hear something I'm going to tell him."

"*Marc!* You're such great buddies, you call him *Marc?*"

Joshua was trapped. What would Charlie do if he knew Marc lived at his house? "He told me to call him Marc. That's his name."

"Well, Gentleman Josh knows how to play his cards, don't he? He's *real* polite and talks *real* smart. He's probably goin' to be a reporter himself someday. So he sneaks into Mr. Mugg's office and cozies up to him and—"

"I do not sneak into his office," Joshua snapped. "For your information, that was the first time I'd ever been there."

"Level with me, kid," said Charlie, moving closer. "What's between you and Mr. Mugg, anyway?"

"Nothing. I heard something I thought he should know. That's all."

Joshua recalled Marc's words: "Charlie acts real tough when he's scared."

"Everything's okay, Charlie," Joshua said reassuringly. "You don't need to worry about me. Honest."

Charlie stepped back. "You on the level?"

"Yes. I'm on the level."

"See that you don't ever double-cross me, Gentleman Josh." Charlie walked away. "Ever."

# AT THE TENEMENTS

THE FRONT PAGE HEADLINES ON THURSDAY'S EVENING edition of the *Traveler* disclosed the breaking story about how Ernest J. Mandeville had been caught embezzling funds from the Jupiter Bank. Joshua was jubilant when he saw the article. He felt even better when Marc slipped a five-dollar bill into his palm that night. Of course, he couldn't have done it without Billy Boot. For a moment Joshua considered splitting the money with Billy. But if he did, he'd have some explaining to do about his arrangement with Marc, so he decided against it.

For the next several days Joshua didn't speak to Charlie, except for a few words when he handed over the money he owed.

Then one morning Joshua arrived for his

papers earlier than usual, just in time to see Charlie and the *Traveler* wagon driver piling newspapers into the handcart. Charlie seemed to be in a hurry.

"Hey, Charlie," Joshua called. "How's Angel's mother?"

"I dunno. I'm headin' down there now to see."

"Can I come with you?" Joshua asked. "It's still early."

Charlie paused. "Oh, all right. Come on," he beckoned.

Joshua pulled the filled wagon back to the alley and then raced down the street to the waiting horse and dray. Charlie pulled Joshua up onto the seat beside him.

Over the clomping of the horse's hooves, Joshua could hear the sound of a boat's horn. The creaks of wooden vessels as they pulled against the dock pilings echoed on the strong east wind. Joshua pulled his jacket collar up around his face. The horse snorted, and steam billowed from its nostrils. The morning was cold and bleak.

Charlie finally spoke. "Listen, I know it was you who got that Jupiter Bank story to Mr. Mugg."

"Who told you that?"

"One of my boys saw you talkin' to Billy Boot," Charlie said. "I've had a good talk with Billy, and he won't be givin' you any more information, you can be sure of that. I thought you got it straight, kid. This is my town. I'm the one who gave you a job. I've been the chief newsie here for two years. And Mr. Mugg is *my* connection. Got it?"

The driver spoke up. "Cut it out, Charlie. Leave the kid alone."

Charlie sank back into the seat. "If we tell Mugg the same story, then it's mine. I get dibs on it. I've got"—Charlie struggled for a word—"*seniority.*"

"So, what does that leave for me?"

"Any story you find on your own is yours, so long as it ain't from one of *my* sources." Charlie scowled at Joshua.

Joshua looked around. "Are we near Angel's house?"

"Over there," Charlie said, nodding in the direction of several tenement buildings.

Joshua had never been this close to tenements before. Across the street, beyond the trestle bridge of the elevated train, the old, wooden buildings stood in a dreary row.

"Which house is hers?" Joshua asked. "They all look alike."

It was impossible to tell what shade of paint the houses might have been at one time. Every house in the vicinity was a dismal gray. The narrow alleys between the houses were filled with overflowing trash barrels.

"That one," Charlie said, pointing to the most run-down of the three-story tenements.

The wagon stopped, and the boys climbed off.

"Wait for us," Charlie said to the driver. "I'm just checkin' to see if Angel will be sellin' her papes today."

The driver shrugged. "Don't take all day, Charlie. I ain't your private chauffeur, you know. I gotta get this gig back to the plant."

Charlie pulled two bags from the back of the wagon. "And I've gotta drop this stuff off," he muttered, not looking at Joshua.

"What is that stink?" Joshua asked, wrinkling his nose.

"Just trash, snob," snickered Charlie. "Ain't you got trash up in your fancy neighborhood?"

But the overpowering smell was not coming from garbage. The wind carried a strange, sickening sweet stench that puckered Joshua's tongue and throat.

Joshua followed Charlie up a pair of rickety steps to a weather-beaten door. Joshua was relieved to get inside the building. Even the musty reek of damp wood that mixed with the scent of toilets wasn't as foul or disgusting as the sickening odor outdoors.

A dark hallway stretched along to the right of a stairway. "Don't they have electricity yet?" Joshua whispered.

Charlie didn't answer as he started upstairs with the two bags in his arms.

Joshua heard someone coughing and stopped on the first landing. "I—uh—I think I'll wait outside," he told Charlie.

"Why, are you scared? Never seen the likes of this?"

"Charlie, they may have influenza. I've already had it, and even though they say you can't get it twice, I'm not going up there." Charlie shrugged and disappeared up the stairway.

Poor Angel, Joshua thought. How can anyone

expect to stay healthy in this place? His mother had warned him to stay away from the tenements. Now he knew why.

Once outside, Joshua climbed onto the wagon. "These houses are awful," he said to the driver. "They don't have electricity."

"That ain't all they don't have," said the man. "Everyone in that building has to share one bathroom."

Joshua shuddered.

"The neighborhood's not as bad it used to be," said the driver. "And there's a nice park just up the way—the North End Playground."

Joshua looked around. Ugly warehouses stood on the other side of the street. A sign read, BOSTON & WORCESTER RAILWAYS. Another building, with a horse barn adjoining it, was marked, PUBLIC WORKS. Closer to the water was a fire station where a fireboat was hitched to the wharf.

A huge steel tank towered above the buildings, casting a shadow on the cheerless neighborhood.

"What's in that tank?" asked Joshua.

"Crude molasses. Can't you smell it?" The

man took out a pipe and stuffed it with tobacco from a leather pouch.

"That's what smells so awful? Molasses?"

"That's it. Doesn't smell like cookies, does it?"

"It's sickening. What's it used for?"

"Rum, I guess. It belongs to the Purity Distilling Company." He turned from the wind, scratched a match on the side of the wagon, then held it to the bowl of the pipe. The tobacco began to glow as the driver inhaled steadily on the pipe. Then he continued, "Can't imagine why they'd store all that molasses with Prohibition so near at hand. It'll be against the law to brew rum if that bill passes." The driver sat back and puffed on his pipe.

"I'd hate to smell that rotten stink all the time," Joshua said. "I'm going to take a closer look while we're waiting for Charlie." He climbed off the wagon and walked under the elevated trestle toward the tank. He wandered over to some firemen who were standing outside the station.

"Excuse me," he said. "Is that tank full of molasses?"

"Yeah, it's molasses, all right. Haven't you seen it before?" asked one of the firemen.

"I've never been down this way. How much molasses does it hold?"

"A few million gallons, they say," another fireman answered.

"What's it for?" Joshua asked.

"They use it to make alcohol for munitions," said a third man. "They haul it off to Cambridge in trolley tank cars. Molasses is a big thing here in Boston."

"It has a big stink, too," said Joshua.

"That's 'cause it leaks. See the molasses oozing out of the seams?" The man pointed to the steel tank. "That thing's gonna blow someday, I swear."

"Well, you'd better not be around here when it does!" The first fireman slapped his friend on the back, and everyone laughed.

Charlie was climbing onto the wagon, and Joshua ran back across the street. "How's Angel?" he asked, getting onto the seat.

"She's okay, but her mother's still sick. I'll have to get someone to sell these papes at her corner," Charlie said almost to himself. "She has a good, safe stand up near city hall. I'll get Shawn to do it."

The driver clicked the reins, and the horse slowly ambled away.

"Hey, what were you doin' across the street?" Charlie asked.

"Just asking about that molasses. What do *you* think it's used for?"

"For Boston baked beans," Charlie said with a smirk. "Don't ya know that Boston baked beans are made with molasses? Or don't you highbrows eat beans?"

"Quit calling me names, Charlie."

"Ta ta! Can't take bein' called a highbrow?"

"Not from an ignoramus like you!"

"Listen to the big shot here. Can't even speak English. There ain't no such word as 'igno . . . ramus.'"

"You're the one who can't speak English," Joshua shot back. "There's no such word as 'ain't'! *Don't say 'ain't.' Your mother will faint. Your father will fall in a bucket of paint!*" Joshua chanted.

The driver pulled on the reins and stopped the wagon. "All right, you kids. If you don't stop this arguin' and fightin' you can both walk back." He waited, then clicked the reins and the horse moved on again.

Joshua settled back. "Let's get out of this place. I can't stand it around here."

"Poor you! You only saw the outsides," Charlie taunted. "The insides are really somethin'. Half the time they ain't even got water. And the rats from the waterfront—"

Joshua interrupted. "People shouldn't have to live like that."

"Oh, la dee da. Where are they gonna live, then? Up in your neighborhood, Gentleman Josh?" Charlie snorted. "They ain't got money. They ain't got jobs that pay anything." Charlie pulled a neatly folded paper from his pocket and shoved it at Joshua. "Here. Angel said for me to give you this."

Joshua opened it. "It's a drawing," he said. "A cartoon. It looks like me!"

Charlie looked over Joshua's shoulder and laughed. "Yep. That's you, all right. Big mouth and all."

The picture was a pencil drawing of Joshua with his canvas bag and soft visored cap. He was riding on a speeding cart full of newspapers. On its side were the words BOSTON TRAVELER.

The newsboy in the picture had his mouth

open wide as if he were hollering out the headlines with all his might. "That's pretty clever," Joshua said. Angelina's name was scribbled on the bottom: ANGELINA DIPIETRO.

"She said somethin' about . . . tryin' to find a way to say thanks for the toy you gave her kid sister, or somethin'," Charlie said, looking ahead at the road.

"Angel is an artist!" Joshua kicked the seat in front of him angrily. "It's not fair! She should be in art school instead of being a newsie in boy's clothes."

"How could she get into a school?" Charlie asked. "They're poor people."

"Maybe she could get a scholarship. I've heard there are scholarships for newsboys." Instantly Joshua regretted his words, but it was too late.

Charlie looked at Joshua suspiciously. "Where'd you hear that?"

"I can't remember. I was only thinking that if people knew how talented Angel is, maybe someone would give her a scholarship. Maybe she'd become famous. Well, at least she might get a job someday and move out of the tenements."

"People like Angel don't stand a chance," Charlie

said with a wave of his hand. "Just forget it."

"Why doesn't the mayor or the governor do something? Why don't they build some decent places for poor people?"

"Why don't *you* get on a soapbox up in the Common and give a speech?" Charlie said with a snort.

"Or write a letter to Governor Coolidge," the driver added.

Joshua ignored their remarks. "I think the tenants should complain."

"If the landlord fixed up these places, the rents would go up and nobody here could afford to live in 'em," the driver explained. "Most of these folks are immigrants. Some don't even speak English."

"I'd sooner die than live here."

"Well, you don't have to, do you?" said Charlie. "You live in a nice, fancy house far away from the slums, so you don't need to worry about nothin.'"

"You think things are easy for me, Charlie?" Joshua blurted. "Do you think I'd be pedaling papers on the streets if I didn't *have* to?"

No one spoke, and for a while the only sound was the clomping of the horse's hooves and the rumble of the wheels. It had begun to snow, and the large flakes filled the air like butterflies.

Then Joshua went on. "Someone should write a news article about these places. Go ahead, Charlie. Tell Mr. Mugg about it. He might pay you something. This should make a good story. Isn't that what newspapers are for? To tell people what's going on?"

"He already knows about tenements. He's from New York City, for cryin' out loud. Tenements ain't nothin' new. They're not *news*," Charlie answered. "He's lookin' for a *big-time* story."

Maybe Charlie was right. No one seemed to care. No one would be interested in Angel or the tenements.

Joshua folded Angel's drawing and placed it carefully in his pocket.

# A MEETING AT ANGEL'S CORNER

IT WAS STILL SNOWING THAT AFTERNOON WHEN Charlie appeared at Joshua's corner on State Street. He was lugging Joshua's afternoon papers in another cart. "I need you to take Angel's place. Just for today. Shawn is takin' another kid's corner this afternoon, so go up to city hall for the rest of the day."

"But, Charlie, my customers here are just getting to know me," Joshua complained. "Nobody knows me up there."

"Do as I say," Charlie ordered. "I'll stick around here and sell my own papes until I run out." He had already pulled Joshua's cart out from the alley and was stacking it with the evening edition.

"But I just got my business started here," Joshua persisted.

"Are you deaf? Do you think State Street will close down 'cause Gentleman Josh ain't here? I told you to go up to city hall. Just go!"

"Why don't *you?*" Joshua shot back before he grabbed the handle of his cart and stormed up the street.

"It's only for today!" Charlie yelled after him. "You don't have to come back to divvy up with me today. Do it tomorrow."

Joshua didn't acknowledge he even heard Charlie. He jerked the cart over the curbing, nearly overturning it.

He crossed Washington Street, headed up the hill to city hall, and posted himself on the sidewalk near the front entrance. It wasn't long before people started filing out of the building and stopped to buy a paper. Joshua could move his hands as quickly as Charlie now—handing out papers and making change as fast as a magician doing card tricks.

Suddenly someone in the street screamed. "Watch out!"

A gray-haired man staggered out in front of an automobile. When the driver blasted his horn, a horse pulling a wagon reared, then bolted forward.

"Whoa! Whoa!" yelled the man on the wagon. But the terrified horse lunged directly toward the elderly man in its path.

Joshua dropped his papers and leaped into the street. He grabbed the man's arm and pulled him to the sidewalk just as the horse galloped by with the out-of-control wagon bouncing behind.

The man teetered on the icy curb. "Are you all right?" Joshua asked, still holding his arm.

"Here, here! I'm fine," the man said grumpily. "Leave me alone, boy."

Joshua stepped back. "I'm sorry, sir. I was afraid you might fall."

The stranger started to walk away, then paused. "Maybe you could . . . help me to that seat?" he asked.

Joshua led the man slowly to a metal bench. He brushed off a dusting of snow, and the man sat down. "Thanks, son," he murmured. "I'm a little unsteady. I've been ill."

"It takes a while to get over it," Joshua said. "Even when you think you've got it beat, it can creep up on you again."

"*It?*" asked the man with a slight frown. "What do you mean, '*it*' can creep up on you?"

"I . . . I just assumed you were recovering from the influenza."

"Assume nothing. Don't you know that a-s-s-u-m-e makes an ass of you and me?"

Joshua nodded. "Sorry, sir. My father died recently from the flu. Just when we thought we all had it licked, his lungs filled with pneumonia."

"Oh, that's a sad shame, son. What kind of work did he do?"

"He was a banker—down on State Street. His name was Jonathan Harper."

"Harper. Of course. I've met him. A promising young man." The gentleman took a long look at Joshua. "So you are his boy—Joshua, isn't it? The lad with the glorious voice? I once heard you sing. What in the name of Sam Hill are you doing on the streets peddling papers? I would assume you'd be at school in the academy. Or better still, studying in the New England Conservatory."

"Assume nothing!" Joshua snapped. Then he bit his lip. He didn't mean to sound rude.

The gentleman seemed taken aback, but then he smiled. "You're right, son. Assume nothing."

"I didn't mean to be impolite," Joshua said.

"It's all right," the stranger replied. "I was a

newsboy once. I had to help out at home, too." He reached out his hand. "I'm John Fitzgerald."

Joshua looked up in surprise. "Mayor Fitzgerald?"

"The *former* mayor," Mr. Fitzgerald corrected him.

"I'm proud to meet you, sir." Joshua shook the man's hand.

"You were right, you know. I am recovering from the influenza. I didn't want the public to know I've had it. That's why I barked at you." He grinned. "My daughter, Rose, says I want people to think I'm invulnerable." Mr. Fitzgerald shook his head. "But I thought I was done for this time."

Joshua sat down on the bench. "I'm taking this corner for a friend today. She's the one who usually sells papers here. Her mother is really sick right now with the influenza."

"Hm. A pretty, dark-eyed girl who dresses in boy's clothes?"

"Yes, that's her. Her name is Angelina. She has to take care of her mother and her little sister. Angel lives in the North End, near that big molasses tank."

"I know the area very well. I used to live near there," Mr. Fitzgerald said. "No place to be if you're sick."

"No place to be if you're *well*," Joshua replied.

"Not everything is terrible in that neighborhood. One of the best things I did as mayor was to build the North End Playground. It's a safe place for children to play. Just up the street from that molasses tank."

"I've heard about it, sir," Joshua answered.

"You're doing a fine thing, helping out your sick friend. When I was a newsboy I had a friend who sold papers, too. His name was Fred. He had a lucrative stand up on Tremont Street. But he got very sick. Tuberculosis. I tried to help out, like you, taking his corner for part of the day. Otherwise someone else would grab his place and he'd lose it for good. He did lose it for good, as it turned out. He died from consumption." The man paused. "He was my best friend."

Joshua had been so angry when Charlie had sent him away from his own corner. But now he knew why Charlie had done it: Angel might lose this profitable, safe place if someone didn't keep it for her.

"I didn't realize anyone could take over a corner just like that," Joshua said.

"Some newsboys can be pretty mean," said the former mayor. "The hawks, we called them."

"I work for Charlestown Charlie. He can be pretty mean. But then, he wanted me here today for Angel. Sometimes I can't figure him out."

"I know Charlestown Charlie. He drops by now and then." Mr. Fitzgerald chuckled. "He seems to keep a tab on everyone in town. He can be tough, but there's a soft side to him, too. How come you're not selling on your own?"

"Charlie found *me* when I was looking for a job. He takes care of everything, especially for us younger kids who are too young to be part of the new union. So he sells loads of papers, and we don't get in trouble."

Mr. Fitzgerald chuckled. "Charlie's got all the answers. I'm not sure they're totally accurate. I used to get down to Newspaper Alley for my papers at three A.M. Sometimes I'd have all mine sold before the regulars even showed up."

"Three in the morning? I live in Back Bay, on Nightshade Lane. My mother wouldn't let me go to work that early. She has no idea that I'm a newsboy," Joshua explained. "She thinks I'm working for the newspaper in 'distribution.'"

"Well, I guess you are, in a way," Mr. Fitzgerald said with a laugh. Then his expression became serious. "You're out of place in this business, Joshua. Selling papers is a tough job, and you're dealing with tough people. It's harder for someone like you who comes from a well-to-do family and has had a different kind of life."

"I don't mind selling papers. I've been thinking of going out on my own, but . . ." Joshua looked down at pigeons that were pecking away at some discarded peanuts.

"You're scared of Charlie." Mr. Fitzgerald nodded.

"He'd probably beat me up. He's warned me enough times."

"If you go on your own, you can make more money than some of the office clerks around here. But you'll have to deal with Charlestown Charlie. He's a struggling kid from a good family. I think he's more of a bluff than a real threat."

"Maybe so." Joshua stood up. "Are you all right

now, Mr. Fitzgerald? I've got to get back to work."

"Yes, thanks, son. I'll just sit here a little while longer and then I'll be on my way." Mr. Fitzgerald reached into his pocket and handed Joshua a dollar bill. "Take this. I've been down in luck myself, and I know what it's like to be newsboy."

"Oh, no sir," Joshua pulled back. "I can't take all that money."

"Sure you can," Mr. Fitzgerald insisted. "You pulled me away from that runaway horse just in the nick of time."

Joshua shook his head. "I couldn't take money for doing that."

"You'll never get rich this way," Mr. Fitzgerald scolded as he put the bill away. "But you're a good boy. Your father would be proud of you. Are you still singing with the choir?"

"No, I'm not. Good-bye, Mr. Fitzgerald." Joshua hurried away.

Back on the sidewalk, he held up a newspaper and waited for customers.

Mr. Fitzgerald had said Joshua's father would be proud of him. But his dad would be even more pleased if Josh stood up to Charlie and started his own business.

That's exactly what I'm going to do, Joshua decided. It's time to break away from Charlestown Charlie.

# SNOWBALL FIGHT!

THE SNOW HAD BECOME HEAVY BY THE TIME JOSHUA'S last copy of the afternoon paper was sold. At least he didn't have to go back and divvy up with Charlie. He was cold and wet, and he decided to take the subway from the Common back to the El station.

As he was crossing Tremont Street, Joshua noticed a crowd of well-dressed boys gathered by a lamppost. Their blaring voices sounded familiar. The Beacon Hill Boys! Kids from the academy! His old friends! The boys were pounding snow into an artillery of snowballs.

They've come to fight the North End kids, Joshua thought eagerly.

Snowball fights were a tradition on the Hill. The Beacon Hill boys would lie in wait for the North Enders to gather their forces and invade the Common. Joshua now knew why Charlie had a chip on his shoulder. He and the other poor kids from the North End resented the wealthy boys from Beacon Hill who had everything.

Joshua recognized a tall boy in a heavy green jacket and woolen hat "Hey, Frankie!" he yelled. "Can I fight, too?"

The boy stopped and peered into the twilight. "Who are you?" he asked.

"It's me. Joshua Harper."

The boys looked at Joshua curiously.

"Hi Josh," said Frankie walking closer. "Where've you been? Kids say you've quit school." Frankie looked Joshua up and down, his eyes resting on the *Boston Traveler* bag around Joshua's shoulders. Joshua had forgotten to tuck it into his pocket. "Are you a *newsboy?*"

Joshua hastily stuffed the bag in his jacket. "Um . . . I was just doing someone a favor today," he said. "A kid whose family is sick."

Some of the other boys had joined Frankie. "You're a newsboy," jeered Robert, one of the class big shots. "Joshua's joined the newsboys!" he yelled to the others.

"Are you going to fight with your *Irish pals*

from the North End?" a boy named Henry taunted.

"I don't have any pals from the North End," said Joshua. "What are you talking about?"

"My father saw you hawking papers down on State Street," said Robert. "Couldn't believe his eyes. He said your dad would roll over in his grave if he knew what's become of the famous singer Joshua Harper."

"Yeah, he's still singing," Henry scoffed. "He's singing out the headlines!"

"Well, at least I've got my own business now," said Joshua.

Henry continued badgering. "Josh is in business—on the street."

"That's more than you'll ever do," Joshua snapped. "The only jobs you'll ever get are the ones your fathers get for you. You couldn't get work anywhere else."

Henry grabbed a snowball from the pile and hurled it at Joshua.

The hard-packed missile hit Joshua in the face. The icy snow smarted his skin, then slipped down his cheeks.

"How'd you like snow in your face?" Henry

laughed. "Or don't newsboys wash their faces?"

Furious, Joshua pounced on the larger boy, knocking both of them to the ground.

Joshua smacked a fistful of snow in Henry's face. "How do you like snow in *your* face!" he yelled.

Henry struggled and punched aimlessly at Joshua, but Joshua sat on his chest and whammed him with more snow.

Henry was starting to cry. "Get him off of me!" he screamed.

Two boys dragged Joshua up by the collar. Joshua yanked away and was about to run off when he heard someone call his name.

"Josh! Over here!" Billy Boot was peeking out from behind a huge granite pedestal of a statue. Stumbling and slipping, Joshua raced toward Billy. Snowballs smashed against his head and back.

Joshua ducked behind the pedestal. A dozen or so kids from the North End were feverishly packing snowballs.

"Am I glad to see you, Billy," Joshua exclaimed, crouching into the hiding place. "I thought those kids were my friends."

"Are you nuts? They ain't gonna be friends with a *newsboy*," Billy said. "*I* shouldn't even be talkin' to you after what you did. Charlie was ready to beat me up for spillin' the beans to you about the Jupiter Bank."

"Aw, forget it, Billy," said Joshua. "You got the Beacon Hill boys to worry about right now. They know you're back here."

"Yeah, thanks *to you!*" Shawn stood above Joshua with his arms crossed. A crowd of North End kids whom Joshua didn't know was standing with him. "We were gonna ambush those bigwigs—but you spoiled everything. You led them right to us."

Joshua struggled to his feet. "I didn't know you were here, Shawn. Let me stay and fight with you guys."

"Oh, no. You're one of *them!*"

Joshua scanned the faces in the shadows. "Where's Charlie? Is he here?"

"He ain't here to take care of *you*. He's got more important things to do." Shawn grabbed Joshua. "Get outta here! Go back to your snotty friends." He shoved Joshua out from the safety of the statue.

Joshua put his hands over his head to ward off a new bombardment of snowballs—this time from both sides. He flung himself behind a stout elm tree. Working quickly, he made a stack of snowballs and shoved them into his *Traveler* bag.

The park was still now as both sides waited for the other to make a move. All Joshua wanted was to go home. The lighted subway station was just beyond the Beacon Hill Boys.

Joshua made a wild dash toward the academy kids, taking them by surprise. "Yahh! Yahh!" he screamed, pulling out the snowballs and hurling them as he raced by. Henry yelped as one hit him directly in the head. Another smashed against Robert's chest.

Joshua felt one last snowball slam against his jacket before he ducked into the safety of the subway entrance.

# THE PARTY

JOSHUA ARRIVED HOME JUST AS THE HEAVY WIND began to drive the snow into high drifts. His mother had put water into the gas log in the parlor and ignited it. The water in the log would heat up to warm the room. It wasn't a real wood fire, but it looked bright and cheerful.

Marc Muggeridge, dressed in a casual smoking jacket, was lighting candles on the mahogany dining table.

Joshua removed his wet coat in the kitchen. He pulled Angel's drawing out of the pocket and unfolded it carefully. The paper was damp, but the picture was clear. Joshua grinned at the caricature and placed the drawing on a side table by his father's chair in the parlor.

Dressed in a floor-length gray velvet gown,

Aunt Caroline descended the stairs cautiously, carrying her cane. "Good evening, Joshua. So glad you could make it home in time. Your mother has planned a lovely dinner for us."

"I'm just going to change into some dry clothes," said Joshua, heading upstairs.

When Joshua returned, his mother was looking out the long parlor window. Her hair fell in gold ringlets over her shoulders. "See how the snowflakes dance in the lamplight? It makes me think of the old days." She sighed. "The old days. That would be only last year. When your father and I entertained, so many people looked forward to our parties." She motioned for Joshua to join her, then put her arm around his shoulder. "Remember?" She pointed to the street. "Remember the chauffeured carriages and automobiles stopping at our gate? Remember the gentlemen in their high-topped hats, and ladies in beautiful gowns? Oh, I do miss your father."

Joshua could think only of the jeers he had received from his so-called academy friends. He hoped the Irish North Enders were knocking them senseless.

His mother rang a little silver bell. "Dinner is served," she said, removing her apron. As Joshua followed the adults into the dining room, he noticed with a start that instead of her usual black mourning attire, she was wearing a cranberry-red silk dress.

Marc held the chair for Aunt Caroline, and Joshua held the chair for his mother.

"Are we having a party?" Joshua asked.

"Aunt Caroline thought it was high time we have an elegant, cheerful dinner," said Mom, passing platters of chicken breasts stuffed with walnut dressing, baked potato, and golden winter squash seasoned with maple sugar and nutmeg.

"I made the rolls," said Aunt Caroline. "It felt good to be doing something for a change rather than sitting in that room all day."

"Everything looks delicious," said Marc, heaping his plate high with food.

"Dinner did come out well, considering I don't have an electric stove like everyone else," said Mom with a sad smile. "The gas stove is so old-fashioned. Someday . . ." She stopped and peered at Joshua from across the table. "Josh, what is that awful red mark on your face?"

"Some ice fell from a . . . roof," he lied.

Marc glanced up at Joshua. "From a roof?"

"And I happened to be looking up . . . um . . . to see if—"

"Yes, one must be careful with icicles this time of year," Aunt Caroline said, ending the discussion.

After a dessert of hot Indian pudding and hard sauce, everyone moved into the parlor.

Mother curled up on the sofa and sipped on coffee while Marc pulled out a pipe and settled himself in Dad's big leather chair.

"Don't sit in Dad's chair," Joshua snapped.

"I'm sorry," said Marc, getting up.

"It's perfectly all right," Mom said quickly. "My husband would want you to be comfortable. He was always a gracious host."

Marc settled back in the chair. Joshua noticed that the side table was empty. Where was Angel's drawing? Would his mother have recognized him in the caricature? He went over to the table to see if it had fallen to the floor. But it was gone.

Joshua sat nervously in a ladder-backed chair

near the window. Aunt Caroline stood by the piano and gently touched the ivory keys.

"Why don't you play for us?" Marc urged her.

"It's been a while." Aunt Caroline slipped onto the bench, held her hands over the keyboard, then began to play. Her gnarled fingers flew over the keys.

Chopin's "Minute Waltz," Joshua thought. I'll bet she could play it in sixty seconds, too. Aunt Caroline was full of surprises.

"I do so enjoy fine music," said Mom. "You play beautifully, Aunt Caroline. It's wonderful to have music in our home again." She stepped over to the piano.

"Here's a popular song," Aunt Caroline began to play and sing a lively tune. "Row, row, row, way up the river he would row, row, row." Marc got up to join in the singing. Aunt Caroline knew many favorite songs. They sang "Beautiful Ohio" and "If I Had My Way, Dear."

"Sing with us, Joshua," Mom begged.

Joshua shook his head.

There was something about the music, though, something magical about the candlelight and the singing. Mom seemed like her old self. And

Joshua couldn't help tapping his foot to the rhythms.

But then Aunt Caroline played "Memories," and Joshua saw the sadness creep back into his mother's eyes.

"Music has a way of toying with my heart," Mom said.

"It was a lovely evening, Gwendolyn," said Aunt Caroline. "Thank you, my dear."

"Ditto," said Marc. "Can I help with anything?"

"No, thank you. I'll clean up in the morning," said Mom, heading for the kitchen. "I'll tend to the furnace and then I'm going to bed."

Aunt Caroline's dress swished and her cane clicked as she went up the stairs. "Good night," she called.

"Good night," Joshua said. He turned to Marc. "I need to talk to you."

Marc nodded. "Come up to my room."

Joshua sat opposite Marc at the oak desk. Marc looked at Joshua's sore face. "Did Charlie beat you up?"

"No, it was some kids I know from school. They used to be friends of mine, but now they don't want anything to do with a *newsboy.*" Joshua shrugged. "The North End kids don't like me, either."

"So what can I do for you, Josh?"

"I'm going into business on my own."

Marc nodded. "I figured as much. Charlie won't be happy."

"Charlie's making money off of me!"

"That's what bosses do. They pay their employees. Charlie's in business and he has employed *you*."

"Well, that's too bad for Charlie, 'cause I've decided to be my own boss."

"You're a good newsboy. People like you. Maybe you'll win a scholarship and go back to school. Even Charlie doesn't want to be a newsboy forever. I'm sure you don't want to, either."

"What else can I do?"

"Maybe you'll be a reporter. You speak the English language effectively, and if you can write as well as you talk, I might buy a *story* from you someday. You'd even have your own byline."

"What's a byline?" Joshua asked.

"It shows the author's name. Yours would say, 'by Joshua Harper.'" Marc reached into the pocket of his jacket and pulled out Angel's picture. "Which reminds me, who did this drawing?"

"A newsgirl. My friend, Angelina DiPietro."
Joshua pointed to the signature at the bottom. "I
thought my mother might have taken it."

"I picked it up because I was sure your mother
would recognize you. Even though it's a caricature, it's a dead ringer for you. This Angelina is
talented. Where does she live?"

"In the tenements on Commercial Street. You
know, near the molasses tank."

"You've been down there?" Marc looked surprised.

"Yes. Those places are awful. I was thinking
you should write a story about how miserable it is
there. Kids like Angel are stuck. She'll never get
out of those slums."

"The tenements are new to you, Josh, but
they've been there for years. It's not big news."

"That's what Charlie said."

"Listen, I've been looking for a trademark for
the paper. I like this boy calling out the headlines
as he zooms along on the *Traveler* wagon." He
grinned. "Can I take it to work tomorrow and
show it to the publisher? If he likes it, we'll buy it
from your friend."

*Money for Angel!* "How much?"

"Fifty simoleons, maybe." Marc put up his hand. "But that's not for sure yet, so don't get your hopes up."

*Fifty dollars!*

"Angel needs money badly. Her mother's sick, so Angel can't work."

Marc nodded. "I'll see what I can do."

Joshua got up to leave, then paused. "I wish I could come up with another big story for you," he said. "But now Charlie's warned me not to talk to Billy . . . er . . . the boy who gave me that information about the Jupiter Bank."

"Just keep your eyes and ears open and you'll find more stories." Marc stood up.

"What do you think Charlie will do when he finds out I'm going to buy my papers directly?"

"He may try to work you over. Watch your back and let me know if I can help. I think you'll do just fine once you get over the hurdles Charlie may set up."

"Thanks, Marc," Joshua replied. "And don't forget about Angel's picture."

Joshua could hardly sleep. He would have to wake up before dawn to get down to Newspaper

Alley. He'd be just like Mr. Fitzgerald. Mom wouldn't like it, but Dad would be proud of him.

One thing was certain, though. It wasn't going to be fun facing Charlestown Charlie.

# JOSHUA BREAKS
# THE NEWS

THE SNOW AND ICE HAD STARTED TO MELT AND THEN froze during the night. Before dawn Joshua got up, filled a bucket of ashes from the cellar, and sprinkled them on the slippery walks. A warm wind, unusual for Boston in January, whistled around the house.

He went back into the kitchen, closing the door quietly behind him. He mustn't wake Mom. She'd wonder why he was leaving so early and ask a million questions.

Marc was there, already dressed. "I heard you getting up," he said.

"Yeah. I decided to face Charlie."

"I'll go in with you, in case you need some moral support." Marc put some coffee and water into the percolator and set it on the stove with a clatter.

"Shh! Don't make so much noise," Joshua whispered. The stove came on with a loud *POP!* "Pipe down, Marc."

Joshua planned to make his own lunch and leave before Mom woke up. He opened the icebox. There were three chicken breasts left over from last night. He'd take them—and that extra bottle of milk—to Angel and her family.

His hands were full, so he slammed the door shut with his foot. Bang!

"Now who's making noise?" Marc whispered.

Joshua wrapped the chicken breasts in waxed paper and fastened them with a rubber band. He took some bananas, a half dozen of Aunt Caroline's rolls, and stuffed everything into a shopping bag.

Mom came into the kitchen, dressed in her dressing gown. "Why are you up so early?" she asked Joshua as she sliced some bread.

"I have things to do in town."

"What things?"

"I made my own lunch," Josh said, changing the subject.

Mom peeked into the shopping bag. "Josh, you'll never eat all this."

"Yes, I will."

"You're going in early, too?" she asked Marc.

The percolator was bubbling. Marc poured himself a cup of coffee and joined Joshua at the table. "Josh has some business at the paper. I thought I'd go with him. I'll introduce him to the proper people at the *Traveler*."

Mom's face brightened. "Wonderful! See, Joshua? It helps to know the right people." She pulled the bread from the toaster and buttered it. "Joshua won't need to work once we sell that land in Revere. It's oceanfront property." Mom handed Marc the plate of toast.

"Thank you. That land sounds valuable." Marc stuffed his mouth and gulped his coffee. "Let's go, Josh," he said, wiping his mustache. "We can talk business on the El."

Joshua grabbed a slice of bread, covered it with jam, and bolted it down quickly.

Mom sighed and shook her head. "Whatever it is you're doing, I hope things go well for you today. Remember to be polite to your employer, Joshua."

"Why, he's known for being polite," said Marc with a quick wink at Joshua. "'Gentleman Josh,' they call him."

Joshua sent Marc a seething look. He jerked on his jacket, slammed his cap over his head, and grabbed the lunch sack.

"What's that bulge in your jacket?" asked Mom.

"Nothing!" Joshua held his lunch over the pocket where his newspaper bag was stuffed.

"Wait for me." Marc took a final gulp of coffee, pulled on his coat, then followed Joshua out to the street.

"Don't call me 'Gentleman Josh' in front of my mother!" Joshua sputtered.

"Don't be so touchy," Marc responded. "She doesn't know it's a street name."

The sidewalks were slushy, and the warmer air on top of yesterday's melting snow caused a bleak fog to rise. The street lamps glowed eerily as the two walked silently to the train station. It was hard to believe it was only the middle of January. It seemed more like a late March day when the last snow of the winter would be melting. Joshua pulled his gloves from his pocket, then changed his mind and put them back.

Finally Marc asked, "Are you coming directly to the paper?"

"Yes," Joshua answered. "I'll buy fifty papers to start. I'd get a hundred, but I don't have a cart."

"I'll find you one. When you get established, and are faithful about your work, the newspaper may drop them off for you each morning."

"They do that for Charlie sometimes," said Joshua. "And they give him rides in the wagon, too."

Marc laughed. "Charlie can talk anyone into anything. He's a real four-flusher."

The El brought Joshua closer to downtown—and closer to Charlie. He suddenly felt sick to his stomach.

Marc noticed Joshua's silence. "Getting nervous?"

"Yeah, wouldn't you be if you had to face Charlie?"

"I sure would."

Joshua got off at Marc's stop—Newspaper Alley.

Although it was still early, the building was alive with lights. Newsboys were lined up in the alley, picking up their stacks of newspapers. Among them was Charlie, piling up bundles of papers onto two carts.

"I'll go with you to help you sign up," Marc offered.

"I can do it myself," Joshua said.

As they approached the line, Charlie looked up. He seemed surprised to see Marc, but when he saw Joshua, his expression hardened.

Instinctively Joshua grabbed Marc's sleeve. "Stay with me while I break the news to Charlie," he muttered.

Charlie pushed his way through the crowd toward Joshua. "What are you doing *here?*" he asked in an accusing voice.

"I've decided to get my own papers from now on."

Charlie looked Joshua up and down, then flicked his head toward Marc. "How come you're with *him?*"

Marc spoke up. "Hey, Charlie. Didn't you know? I'm his uncle Marc. I live at his house."

"You're his *uncle?* Since when?"

Marc put his arm around Charlie's shoulder, but Charlie pulled away. "Look, Charlie," Marc said. "Josh has every right to sell papers himself. You know that."

"I set him up and put him on my best street.

This is how he thanks me?" Charlie's voice was shaking.

"I won't bother you. I'll just stay on my corner and mind my own business," Joshua promised. "If I hadn't met you, I probably would have done it on my own, anyway. Besides, I need the money, Charlie."

"Yeah, sure you do. Gentleman Josh, the society boy, needs money," said Charlie bitterly.

"Joshua's dad passed away last year. His mother's taking in boarders. That's how I came to live there," Marc explained. "It hasn't been easy for them."

"You *really* live with him?" Charlie turned and glared at Joshua. "I just paid for your papers. Now what am I supposed to do with them?"

"I'll pay you for them. After today I'll get them myself."

"I guess you'll be giving Mr. Mugg here all the good stories, too," Charlie said.

"You know more about what's going on than I do," said Joshua. "You can still find news for Mr. Mugg . . ."

"Of course you can," said Marc. "Our arrangement isn't changing, Charlie."

"Yeah, says you," Charlie muttered. "Go tell it to Sweeney."

"I mean it, Charlie," said Marc. "I want to help you write, too. Nothing has changed. Besides, Josh here doesn't know the ropes about Beantown like you do. Leave Josh alone. He's had a tough time losing his dad. There's a lot of stuff going on with him that you're not aware of. So back off. Okay?"

"Okay, kid," Charlie said with a shrug. "Go ahead, sell your own papes. I'll find some other chump to take your place." As he walked away he called, "I don't need you, anyway."

"See, Josh? Charlie will get over it," Marc whispered. "Give me your lunch bag. You go order a hundred daily papers and I'll get you a cart." Marc disappeared into the crowd.

Joshua made his way to a window where a worker tossed out bundles of papers to the newsboys. "I want to sign up for a hundred copies of each edition," said Joshua, "to start."

"Fill this in," said the workman, shoving a form and pencil toward him. Joshua filled it in and handed it back.

As the man glanced over the form, he whistled.

"*Nightshade Lane?* You live on *Nightshade Lane?*"
He looked Joshua over from head to foot. "How
the mighty have fallen!" he declared. "Do you
need papers today?"

"No, sir," said Joshua.

"Collect your papers here every morning at
this time. The evening editions are ready by two
in the afternoon."

Joshua spotted Charlie putting his stacks of
papers into one of the horse-drawn wagons.

"Hey, Charlie," he called, running alongside.
"I'll buy my share of the papers from you now.
Oh, I almost forgot. I owe you money from yesterday. We didn't divvy up last night." He pulled
coins from his pocket and counted them.

Charlie held out his hand, and Joshua
dropped the change into his palm. Charlie
checked the money and stuffed it into his pocket.
Then he hoisted a stack of a hundred bound
newspapers off the wagon and flung them at
Joshua's feet.

Joshua picked up the heavy bundle of papers
and struggled off with them.

Marc appeared, pulling a wagon behind him.

"You can pick up a cart over in that shed when you need one. Just be sure you sign it out and return it."

Joshua packed his papers in the wagon. "Where are you going to work?" Marc asked, handing him the lunch sack. "State Street?"

Joshua crammed the bag into the cart and pulled on his gloves. "I have customers there," he said. "I'll be okay at my corner. Charlie can't do much to me right in the middle of State Street."

"Good luck. You know where I am if you need me," said Marc as Joshua headed up the wet cobblestone street, pulling the rattling cart behind him.

# TROUBLE IN
# THE WIND

JOSHUA READ THE DAY'S HEADLINES: **"FORMER MAYOR JOHN FITZGERALD RECOVERING FROM INFLUENZA."** Joshua knew that firsthand. The national headlines had to do with the proposed constitutional law prohibiting the manufacture of alcoholic beverages.

**"SIX MORE STATES RATIFY THE AMENDMENT!"** screamed the headlines. **"NATION PREDICTED TO BE DRY BY JULY FIRST."** People who blamed broken homes and crime on "Demon Rum" would be elated if the law was passed. Owners of bars and taverns that lined the Boston Streets would lose their businesses. Yes, this was big news.

"SIX MORE STATES RATIFY PROHIBITION," Joshua bellowed. "NATION WILL BE DRY BY JULY FIRST!"

People lined up to buy papers.

"I'm going to stock up on wine," one banker said to another as they glanced over the first page. They each handed Joshua a dime and said, "Keep the change."

"NATION IS GOING DRY! PEOPLE STOCKING UP ON WINE!" Joshua yelled.

A well-dressed matronly woman bought a paper and counted out exactly three cents. "At last!" she said. "Demon Rum will be off the streets." She smiled at Joshua, then, after rummaging through her small leather purse, she handed him a nickel. "Go celebrate. Buy something nice for your mother."

"This is mighty bad news for me," a man groaned. Joshua recognized him as the well-known owner of the Boston Tavern. "I'll be out of business for sure." He handed Joshua a nickel and waited for the change.

"Those goody-goods in New Hampshire voted for prohibition!" someone muttered.

"NEW HAMPSHIRE VOTES FOR PROHIBITION!" Joshua called.

All of Joshua's papers were sold within an hour.

Joshua sat on the back steps of the bank and

pulled out a piece of chicken from his lunch bag. No, he decided, putting it back. He'd save all of it for Angel, Maria, and their mother. Instead, Joshua ate a roll and a banana. Then he tugged on his gloves, picked up the lunch bag, and headed toward the North End, leaving the cart in the alley.

It was getting warmer. The fog had lifted in the bright sun. The front doors of Faneuil Hall were open, and the gilded copper grasshopper weathervane on the cupola glistened in the sunshine. An orchestra was playing the *Pathetique*, a symphony by Tchaikovsky that Joshua recognized. He decided to go inside the hall. Just for a minute.

Joshua peeked into the Great Hall where a group of musicians were playing on the stage. It was the Amphion Orchestra that had accompanied the Boston Boys' Choir many times.

Joshua removed his cap and gloves and took a seat near the rear of the hall. There was no one else in the audience. The powerful music drifted and echoed through the building.

The symphony was loud, pulsating, forceful.

The pounding of the drums reminded Joshua of ocean breakers rising and crashing in gale winds. Brass horns blared and trumpeted. He leaned back and closed his eyes. Joshua remembered seeing his father's broad smile from the audience when Joshua sang with the choir in this very place. After, his father would say in his quiet, deep voice, "Well done, son!"

The music subsided to pianissimo, and faded to almost silence.

Now the strings took up a new strain as an indescribably peaceful melody filled the auditorium.

Aunt Caroline's words echoed with the lovely, melodious theme. "As long as there is music within me, I'm never alone."

The symphony ended. Members of the orchestra talked and laughed as they gathered up their music and stands.

Outside, the sharp scent of molasses was heavy on the warm wind. At Haymarket Square, a man with a cart was selling hot sweet potatoes

"Smell the molasses?" Joshua asked the vendor.

"I smell it sometimes when there's a north

wind, but it sure seems stronger today. I think a tanker came in recently and filled it." The vendor poured melted butter into a dish. "The thing is supposed to be sealed tight."

Joshua set his bag on the sidewalk, bought a potato, and doused it with melted butter and brown sugar. "Molasses is oozing from the seams."

"The stink isn't good for my business," the man complained.

Joshua wolfed down the hot potato, then headed to the North End. Along Salem Street, little shops featuring Italian groceries lined the narrow road. Skinned rabbits were hanging on display in the windows along with garlands of dried green and red peppers and mushrooms. Bottles of wine glimmered like rubies among various cheeses and breads.

Before heading down Copps Hill to Commercial Street, Joshua gazed toward the city skyline. The hands on the Custom House Tower Clock pointed to noon. No need to rush. The afternoon papers wouldn't be ready for a couple of hours.

Joshua finally arrived in Angelina's neighborhood. Across the street from Angel's house was a line of freight cars on the spur tracks of the Boston & Worcester freight terminal. Melting icicles hung from the rooftop of the Fire Boat 31 Headquarters and sparkled like crystals. Horses whinnied inside the stable next to the Public Works Department. Outside the fire station, firemen in their shirtsleeves were enjoying the pleasant morning.

Joshua crossed under the El train trestle. A train thundered overhead, shaking the ground and rattling windows. He walked up the steps and into the gloomy hallway of Angel's tenement. He could hear voices and someone coughing as he climbed the long wooden stairway. On the third floor he chose one of two doors, and knocked.

"Who's there?" Angel's voice.

"It's me. Josh."

In a few moments the door opened. "Hi, Josh. What are you doin' here? Come in."

Joshua hesitated, still fearful of the dreaded influenza. He stepped into a dim hallway.

Angel turned on a gas light. "This place hasn't been wired for electricity yet," she said apologetically. "Someday we want to live on the west side of the house, so we'll face the afternoon sun. But the rent's higher there."

Angel looked pale in the lamplight. Her dark eyes seemed larger than usual. Joshua was surprised to see how long her hair was. Usually it was tucked up under a hat, but now it fell to her shoulders in curls. Joshua was also startled to see she had on a black skirt and a cream-colored sweater that looked handmade.

"You look right nice, Angel," said Joshua.

"Charlie brought these for me the other day. They were his sister's clothes," Angel said shyly.

Charlie brought clothes for Angel?

Maria came into the room and hid behind Angel's skirt. She peeked out at Joshua, sucking her thumb and clutching the penny doll in her other hand.

"How's your mother?" Joshua asked Angel.

"Her fever has broken, but she's still very weak."

Angel led Joshua down the hall to a parlor where a thin woman lay on a threadbare couch. "This is my mama," Angel said. "Mama, this is Joshua. He works for Charlie, too."

"Good morning, Joshua." Mrs. DiPietro spoke softly in an Italian accent. "I have been ill. Please excuse our humble home." She burst into a series of racking coughs.

"I heard you were sick, Mrs. DiPietro. I brought you something to eat." Joshua offered the sack to Angel.

"Thank you," Angel said, peering into the contents. "It smells so good."

"Chicken," said Joshua. "There's a bottle of milk in there, too."

"I'll get you a plate right now, Mama," Angel said. "You need good food to get well." She disappeared into the kitchen.

Maria climbed onto the couch, leaned against her mother's arm, and smiled at Joshua timidly.

Joshua looked around at the neat, but shabby room. On a nearby table was a drawing pad and some pencils. "I have some good news, Angel," he said when she came back with a tray for her mother.

"You do?" She set the tray on the table next to the sofa.

"A friend of mine saw the drawing you did—the cartoon of me on the wagon. He's going to show it to his boss at the newspaper. They're looking for a picture like that to use as a trademark. He said they might buy it from you."

"Buy it from me? How much would they pay?"

"I don't know. Maybe fifty dollars."

Angel turned to her mother. "Did you hear that, Mama? The newspaper might buy my drawing!"

"Fifty Dollars!" Mrs. DiPietro beamed. *"Basta con le cose cattive! Finalmente tutto va bene!"*

"She said, 'Finally good things are happening.' It's been so hard since Papa went away . . ." Angel's eyes were bright with tears.

"Papa will come back as soon as he's better," her mother said consolingly. "And there's a chance he'll have a job soon. Now, Angelina, I'm going to sit here and enjoy this delicious chicken. Why don't you and Joshua take Maria for a walk in the sunshine. It's such a nice day."

"Will you be all right?"

"I'll be fine. Go up to the playground. It will be good for all of you."

Angel pulled on a jacket and helped Maria into a sweater and hat. "Do you have time? Will Charlie mind if you don't get back soon?"

"I don't work for Charlie anymore," Joshua told her. "I'm working for myself now. I told Charlie this morning."

"Oh, Josh, I hope Charlie doesn't do something mean."

"I'll be okay," Joshua said quickly.

"It's so warm and windy today. It's like spring!" Angel exclaimed when they got to the street. "But the smell of molasses is strong."

"They filled the tank this week," Joshua explained.

A woman was hanging blankets out to air beside a big brick house. "Good morning, Angelina," she called out. "Good morning, Maria. Is your mama better?"

"Yes, she's better, thank you, Mrs. Clougherty," Angel called back.

A striped tiger cat approached them and rubbed against Joshua's legs. "Hello, Peter," Angel crooned. Maria bent down to pat him.

As they walked slowly up the street they passed a policeman. "Good mornin' to ya, Angelina," he said.

"Hello, Officer McManus," Angelina answered.

"Do you know *everyone?*" asked Joshua.

"Practically everyone. This is a nice, friendly neighborhood."

At the entrance of the North End Playground, they could see the water and the Navy Yard in the distance. The harbor glistened with blue and silver waves. Now that they were away from the shade of the molasses tank, the sun was bright. Maria whimpered and put her hands over her eyes.

"We've been inside for so long, the sunshine hurts," Angel explained.

The playground was crowded with children. Angel put Maria on a whirl-around and gave it a push. The little girl laughed for the first time since Joshua had met her.

"This park is a nice place. No wonder Mr. Fitzgerald is proud of it," said Joshua.

"My papa wrote me a letter from Providence," Angel said. "He told me he was proud of me. He's sad he can't be here to help us. I miss Papa."

"I miss my dad, too," Joshua said. "I'll *never* see him again."

"He'd be real proud of you, Josh," said Angel.

"There's one thing I always wanted, and now it's too late. I wish Dad and I could have gone to the top of the Custom House Tower. He went up there once when the tower was first built. He promised he'd take me there sometime, but we never got to go."

"Your papa musta been a real important man. Charlie says they don't let ordinary people like newsboys up to the very top," said Angel.

"Dad said you can see all the way to the foothills of New Hampshire from the observation deck."

"The city must be pretty from way up there. Like bein' in an aeroplane," Angel said. "Maybe you'll go up in the tower someday, Josh."

"It wouldn't be the same without Dad. Nothing's the same without him."

"That's how I feel, too," said Angel. "But my papa is comin' back sometime. I hope."

A shadow fell suddenly over the bench where Joshua and Angel were sitting.

*"Well, if it ain't Gentleman Snob!"*

# EXPLOSION!

"Hi, Angel," said Charlie, not looking at Joshua. "My ma and my sister sent over more stuff they thought you could use. I saw your mama. She said you'd be here."

Angel nodded nervously. "Thank your family for us."

Charlie turned to Joshua. "What a nice day for an outing in the park," he said bitingly. "Now that you're your own boss you can take off whenever you feel like it, right?"

"Come on, Charlie. I told you why I had to go on my own. I need the money."

"Listen, pip-squeak, I've got more bones to pick with you. Today I dropped in on Mr. Fitzgerald. And what does he say to me? He says, 'I met one of your boys, Joshua Harper. He's a nice kid.

You take good care of him, okay, Charlie?'" Charlie shoved his face close to Joshua's. "So now you're gettin' in tight with Mr. Fitz. And just what are you tellin' him about me?"

Joshua backed away. "I never said anything bad about you, Charlie."

"You keep on pushin' your way into my territory. First, playin' up to Mr. Mugg, and now Mr. Fitzgerald. After all I done for you!" Charlie grabbed Joshua's collar and dragged him to his feet.

"Oh, go chase yourself!" Joshua barked, pulling himself away from Charlie's clutch.

"Here's a knockout punch that'll fix you once and for all, *Gentleman* Josh!" Charlie socked Joshua in the chest, knocking him to the ground.

Angel stood up and screamed, "Stop it, Charlie!"

Because of his heavy jacket, Charlie's blow didn't hurt that much. Joshua picked himself up and was about to wallop Charlie, but Charlie swatted him down again. Maria started to cry and as she struggled to get off the whirl-around, she slipped and fell to the pavement. Angel picked her up, but the little girl's mouth was bleeding.

"Look what you've done now, Charlie!" Angel yelled.

"Aw, I ain't done nothin'—yet!"

"I'm going to get Officer McManus," Angel exclaimed. "Come on, Josh." She headed for the street, struggling to carry her screaming sister.

Joshua got up, put his cap back on, and followed her. Angel crossed under the El trestle and marched toward Officer McManus, who was standing at a nearby call box.

"Whatsa matter?" Charlie yelled after them. "Afraid to fight?"

Joshua was tempted to turn around and bash Charlie. Instead, he yelled, "Oh, go fly a kite, Charlie! I don't want to fight anyone!"

"Come back here!" Charlie started after Joshua.

RAT-A-TAT-A-TAT-TAT-TAT!

"What's that? It sounds like a machine gun!" Officer McManus yelled.

RAT-A-TAT-A-TAT-TAT-TAT!

Suddenly a thunderous *BOOM!* shook the earth and echoed through the street. With a deafening, sucking noise, a blast of hot wind enveloped the neighborhood. Dirt and debris whirled around like a cyclone. CRASH! The sounds of breaking glass and the clatter of toppling houses echoed in the streets. Joshua's cap flew off his head and blew away. He clapped his hands over his popping ears.

"Is it an earthquake?" Joshua yelled.

"A tornado!" someone else hollered.

WHIR! A huge piece of steel hurtled through the air and slammed into the supporting column of the train trestle. The brace snapped like a toothpick, and the tracks dropped into the street with an enormous CRASH!

Screaming, Angel pulled Maria to the ground and threw herself on top of her. Children and grown-ups came running and shrieking from the playground.

Racing behind Joshua, Charlie yelled, "It's the tank! The molasses tank is exploding!"

"Run! Get up the hill quickly!" Officer McManus bellowed. "Run!" He grabbed the telephone from the call box and rotated the handle. "Send all available ambulances, all police, everybody!" he roared into the signal box. "The tank has blown!

There's a wall of molasses coming down Commercial Street!"

Joshua and Charlie pulled Angel and Maria to their feet. They all dashed to the side street and up Copps Hill. A deep gurgling sound like thunder followed them.

Angel tripped, almost dropping her sister. Charlie grabbed Maria and hoisted her onto his shoulders. When they were near the top of the hill, they turned.

"Holy Mary, mother of God!" Charlie gasped.

A tidal wave of yellowish-brown molasses was gushing from the broken tank and barreling over the streets. Automobiles, trucks, and wagons were lifted high and sucked down into the sticky sludge.

"There's Anthony di Stasio comin' home from school!" Angel screamed. "Run, Anthony!" she called to the boy, waving frantically.

Anthony looked back at the wall of molasses, then tried to outrun it, but the giant wave picked him up on its crest, then as it toppled forward, Anthony vanished.

Men in wagons whipped their frantic horses,

trying to get away, but they were quickly trapped in the deepening sea of syrup.

The screams of victims, the clatter of wagons, the roar of the escaped molasses mingled with the cries of the onlookers. *"Hurry! Watch out! It's coming closer!"*

The gooey mass swept forward like lava, engulfing everything in its path. A screaming horse and carriage overturned. Joshua could see the horse's legs sticking out of the mire, then both carriage and horse sank into the shiny liquid.

The great wave of molasses roared its way to the base of Copps Hill, where it surged up another fifteen feet. "The molasses smashed right through Mrs. Clougherty's brick house!" one of the bystanders on the hillside yelled.

The sharp snap of steel girders and ripping wood rebounded everywhere. Horses dropped to their knees, then disappeared into the gluey muck.

Angel pointed toward the El. "Look! There's a train comin'! But there's no track left! If it don't stop, it'll crash."

They watched helplessly as the elevated train clattered directly toward the broken trestle.

"Stop!" Charlie yelled.

"They can't hear you." Joshua jumped up and down, waving his hands wildly. Other people began waving and signaling, too.

"He's slowin' down," said Charlie. "He must've seen us."

The train screeched to a stop only a few feet before the crushed trestle, where the broken tracks swung down to the molasses-filled street

A crowd had gathered on the hill. "The machine gun sounds must have been the rivets popping," a man said. "Then the whole tank blew."

"We've got to help those people!" a woman yelled.

"How?" someone asked. "We'd be sucked right into the molasses."

"It's destroying everything!"

The massive tide hurled loaded freight cars through the iron walls of the terminal. The deadly liquid wove its way into basements and alleys, rising higher and higher to the second and third floors, until some of the buildings gave way and collapsed.

"It's heading for the wharves!" Charlie said.

The fire station toppled on its side in the great surge of molasses, and the shattered building was being carried toward the ocean.

Where are the firemen? Joshua wondered in panic.

"Mama! I've got to save Mama!" Angel screamed and started to run down the hill, but Charlie grabbed her. "You can't go down there. Stay here with Maria. Josh and I will go see what's happened to your house." He thrust Maria to Angel, and the two boys raced down toward the sea of churning molasses.

"What'll we do when we get there?" Joshua called to Charlie. "We can't get through that stuff! It's up to the second story of the Public Works. We could get swallowed up in it."

"We'll just get close enough to see Angel's house. There's nothin' else we can do."

The biting stench of molasses was nauseating, and the taste of molasses was thick on Joshua's tongue.

He and Charlie pushed their way through the crowds and leaped over the scattered debris. From windows, people screamed for help. Horses floundered in the molasses near the stables across the street. "Help us!" screeched clerks from the upper floors of office buildings.

"Oh, dear God," Joshua prayed aloud. "Can't we help those people?"

Charlie shook his head. "There's no way. We can't cross through. It's like quicksand. We'd be sucked right in and drown."

The boys stopped, unable to go any farther. The deep lake of molasses swelled and churned under the broken trestle.

Angel's house was partially caved in. The first two floors had buckled under the wave of molasses. The third story was sitting precariously on top of the rubble, about ready to topple.

"Charlie, Mrs. DiPietro might still be alive in there."

"There's someone in the window!" Charlie yelled.

A figure was standing and gesturing wildly through the broken glass. "Help!" Her faint cries could barely be heard over the wailing of other victims and the shrieks of dying horses.

"We've got to help Angel's mom," Joshua cried.

"How can we get to her?"

"Let's go back up the hill. Maybe we can approach the house from the other side."

The two boys ran back to where Angel waited. She was kneeling by Maria, attempting to calm her.

"We're going to try to help your mother," Joshua explained breathlessly. "The house is caving in, but maybe we can get there in time."

"Oh, please help Mama," Angel begged. Tears streamed down her face as she crossed herself. "*O Dio mio!*"

The boys headed down to the other side of the hill only to discover the molasses had totally surrounded Angel's tenement. They watched as pieces of the house broke and dropped into the gluey liquid. A table floated by, then a door. The more the molasses churned, the more the buildings collapsed, releasing broken windows and stairways into the sticky mess.

"I have an idea," said Joshua. "There's junk all over. Maybe I can crawl from one piece to another until I reach the house.

"Then what?" Charlie asked. "Even if you don't sink into the molasses, the house could cave in, anyway."

Joshua pointed to a long, wooden ladder that must have broken away from the fire station. He took off his jacket, tossed it onto a broken post, then stepped into the sludge. He waded up to his waist in the molasses, praying he wouldn't step into a hole. The deeper he went, the more the molasses seemed to paralyze his legs so each step became a struggle until—WHOP!—the molasses sucked off both of his boots! His socks were matted and soggy as he staggered toward the ladder.

Something bumped into his leg—something floating deep in the molasses. He reached down and pulled it to the surface. A cat! It was covered with the slimy syrup, but Joshua could make out the tiger stripes around the face. Peter! Gagging, he thrust the animal aside.

What else was under that awful sludge? Cringing with every step, Joshua climbed onto a broken stairway that wobbled dangerously. At the furthermost point he reached out to the ladder and pulled it toward him.

Charlie clambered after Joshua. "Careful," Joshua said. "The molasses is going to get deeper the closer we get to the house."

"I'll stay behind you," said Charlie. "We can't get on the junk out there together, 'cause if one of us don't sink, two of us *will*."

"Hey! You kids!" a man yelled. "Don't go out there! It's dangerous!"

But the two boys set the ladder on top of some wood, then aimed it to another piece of lumber closer to the crumbling tenement.

"I'll hold it steady while you climb out there," Charlie said.

Joshua lay down on the ladder and began his slow crawl over the rungs toward the house. His clothes, coated with molasses and dirt, stuck to his body and to the ladder, and each motion was stiff and painful. The ladder rocked dangerously. Slowly, he moved to the next rung—then the next—until he finally reached the scrap wood at the front end. Joshua scrambled onto the tippity board. "Come on, Charlie!" he called.

"We're almost there," said Charlie.

Joshua aimed the ladder toward another piece of lumber, then continued crawling toward the tenement. The film of molasses in his throat sent him into a fit of coughing, and he paused before moving on. He looked up once toward the broken window. Mrs. DiPietro wasn't there. Joshua finally reached the house with Charlie right behind him.

The porch and the two lower stories of the tenement had collapsed and were submerged. But the roof of the porch was still attached to the front wall of the building. The two boys slid the end of the ladder to the porch roof and crawled off.

After they secured the ladder to the roof, Joshua crept through shattered glass to the broken window. "Ouch! I've cut my hands," he muttered. He wiped the blood on his sticky shirt, then stood up. "Mrs. DiPietro?" he called. No answer. "I'm going in," he said to Charlie. "Stay out here until I see what's happening inside."

"Be careful, kid," Charlie said. "The floors are probably gone in there."

Joshua cleared away more broken glass, then

crawled cautiously through the wide window opening, wary of cutting his shoeless feet. Inside he recognized some of the furniture, but it was all scattered and smashed. Gingerly, he stepped over the debris to where the living room had been. The outer walls were crushed, and the room was open to the stairway that descended to the molasses. Outside, Red Cross ambulances had already gathered on the side of Copps Hill. People were rushing around, carrying slime-covered victims on stretchers to the waiting vehicles.

"Oh, no!" Joshua gasped. Mrs. DiPietro was caught between boards and plaster on the stairway. "Mrs. DiPietro?"

The woman's eyes fluttered open. *"Dio mio."*

"It's me. Joshua. I've come to help you. Can you move at all?"

"I thought I could go out down the stairs, but the walls caved in," she whispered. "I cannot move."

"I'm going to try to get you out of here," Joshua told her. "I'll need to free you from this plaster and wood."

"It's no use," Angel's mother mumbled. "Too heavy."

She was right. There was no way Joshua could release her from the huge partitions and beams that pinned her to the stairway. "Try to hold on," he said. "I'll send Charlie for help."

He crept back to the window, keeping himself low to the floor as the house pitched around him like a boat in a storm. "I found her, Charlie. She's alive, but she's trapped between walls and beams. The building is wide open on the other side, but the molasses is deep there. This is the only way we can get in and out."

"I'm comin'," Charlie said, swinging one leg over the windowsill.

"No, the house is about to collapse. You've got to get help. Someone should be able to help us."

Charlie moved back and set the ladder onto the cluttered surface of the molasses. "What about you?"

"I'll stay with her. She shouldn't be alone."

"I'll bring help, Josh," Charlie promised, creeping out onto the wobbling ladder.

The house began to tremble, then shake violently. CRASH! The floor was breaking away! Joshua had no choice but to go back to Mrs.

DiPietro. She needed him. Besides, with the ladder gone there was no longer a way for him to escape.

"Oh, my God," Joshua gasped. The stairway had given way and was held up by only one beam! Mrs. DiPietro had fallen with the stairs, and her feet were only inches above the churning molasses.

*God, please be with us*, he prayed.

Joshua inched as near to Mrs. DiPietro as he dared, and reached down for her hand. "Hang on! Charlie is going to get help. Everything will be all right," he said, trying to smile.

"*Dove sono i miei piccini?*" Mrs. DiPietro asked in panting breaths. "Where are Angelina and Maria?"

"They are safe up on Copps Hill."

Mrs. DiPietro breathed heavily. "I know I die, Joshua," she whispered. "Can you bring someone to pray over me?"

"No! You're not dying. You're going to be fine," Joshua said, squeezing her hand. "Angel and Maria are just up the street waiting for you." He pointed out to the blue sky, where the walls had been. "See how the sun is shining and the sky is blue?" He tried to make a little joke. "You've always wanted to be on the sunny side of this house."

Mrs. DiPietro managed a faint smile. "You're a good boy," she muttered.

"I'll go see if Charlie has found anyone to help." Outside, a strange silence drifted across what once was the street. The noise and chaos had given way to an eerie stillness—the way sounds are muffled under a blanket of snow. Occasionally a shot rang out. Someone was probably shooting the trapped, suffering horses that could not be rescued. Other than an occasional call for help, a hush permeated the whole area. Even the lake of molasses was quieter now as the liquid began to settle. The harbor, where the molasses had rammed wharves into the sea, was still and stained an ugly yellow.

Charlie was standing on the side of Copps Hill, gesturing frantically to a group of men. Then they all headed toward the tenement pulling a makeshift stretcher of poles and blankets.

"They're coming!" Joshua called to Mrs. DiPietro. "Charlie's bringing help!"

When he returned to Mrs. DiPietro, she

reached out her hand and Joshua grasped it. "*Sto morendo, prega per me*," she pleaded. "I'm dying, Joshua. I need you to pray for me."

What kind of prayer could he say for this woman he didn't know? She was probably Catholic, but he didn't know how Catholics prayed.

"Pray for me. Ask God to find me here and be with me in the hour of my death," Mrs. DiPietro begged.

His father's favorite hymn, "A Prayer to the Good Shepherd," was a song and a prayer, too. Maybe if Joshua just asked, God *would* be with them. God *would* hear his song.

He held tightly to Mrs. DiPietro's hand, took a deep breath, and began to sing.

"Oh God, my faithful Shepherd,

hear the prayer of this lost sheep;

Come find me on the hillside, and bring me to thy keep.

The vale of death surrounds me,

as the dark'ning shadows fall,

The path is steep and rocky. Good Shepherd, hear my call."

His song—clear and melodious—floated over the silence.

"Hark now, I hear his footsteps, and his gentle voice is near.
   Look, I am with you always. There is no need to fear."

*"Dio mio, non mi lasciare."* Mrs. DiPietro's hand clutched Joshua's even more tightly.

He sang louder, letting the words drown out his own fears.

"He binds my wounds with balsam,
   and his words such comfort bring,
That they heal my broken spirit,
   and cause my heart to sing."

*"Canta per me,"* pleaded Mrs. DiPietro. "Sing, Joshua."

And he let the music pour.

"In loving arms I'm gathered. To the fold he carries me;
Safe in the care of my Shepherd, I shall dwell eternally."

Mrs. DiPietro's hand slackened in Joshua's, and he began to cry.

# A SONG IN
# THE CITY

JOSHUA WAS HUDDLED OVER THE FALLEN STAIRCASE,
clutching Mrs. DiPietro's hand, when Charlie and
two other men crawled into the shattered tenement.

"It's too late," Joshua sobbed. "She's dead."

Charlie bent over him. "Hey, pip-squeak," he
whispered. "Come on. We've got to get you out of
here."

"I can't leave her," Joshua cried.

"Aw, there's nothin' you can do anymore, kid.
You did everything you could." Charlie's voice was
shaking, and tears streamed down his face.

"I couldn't help her. I was right here and I
couldn't do a thing."

"You were with her, kid. That was somethin',
wasn't it?" Charlie leaned down and unclasped
Joshua's fingers from Mrs. DiPietro's grasp. He

put his hands under Joshua's shoulders and pulled him up.

The two men stood nearby with the stretcher. "You're a brave lad," one said, patting Joshua's back. "Now get out while you can, before this whole place collapses."

Charlie urged Joshua out onto the ladder and back into the stinking sea of molasses. "Come on, Josh," he said. "I'm right behind you. Keep goin'."

Joshua did as he was told.

Marc had arrived on the scene with photographers and was standing halfway up Copps Hill. When he caught sight of Joshua and Charlie, he rushed over. "Thank God you're both okay. You sure had us worried." He wrapped his jacket around Joshua's shoulders. "We've got to get you home."

"I lost my shoes," Josh said wearily. He looked around at the seething crowd. People encased in molasses and blood were being taken off in ambulances.

One boy held his hand to his bleeding mouth. "My teeth are gone!" he was crying. "My arm hurts. Where's my sister?"

A nurse in a Red Cross uniform was standing nearby. "That poor lad was on his way home from school when the molasses struck," Joshua heard her tell a police officer. "His sister was killed."

"Where's Angel? I can't tell her that her mama died." Joshua began to weep again.

"Don't cry, kid." Charlie's voice was trembling. "I'll tell her. I'll take care of everything. She and Maria are gonna stay at my house for now." He wiped his nose on his sleeve. "Don't you worry about it, Josh." Charlie nodded to Marc, then walked off.

Marc helped Joshua to one of the taxis that waited at the top of Copps Hill, high above molasses-filled Commercial Street. "I'm going home with you," he said, climbing in beside Joshua.

Joshua put his head back, closed his eyes, and tried to push away the scenes of horror that swirled in his brain.

When they arrived home, Marc led Joshua into the house.

His mother appeared in the hall and began to scream, "Josh! Josh! Oh, my God!"

"He's all right," Marc said soothingly. "There was a terrible explosion in town—"

"An *explosion?*" Mom's voice rose. She reached out to touch her son, then pulled her hands away. "He's covered with . . . molasses! What on earth happened?"

"I'll explain later. But first, get him into a warm tub," Marc ordered.

Later, after his bath, Mom helped Joshua into pajamas, then sat on his bed and put bandages on his cuts. When she was finished she tucked him in with a quilt. "Sleep now," she said, kissing him.

The sound of creaking wagon wheels and clinking bottles broke through Joshua's dreams. The milkman's horse neighed softly in the alley beneath the window.

"No!" He sat up in bed as the memories of the day before startled him awake. Mrs. DiPietro had died and he could do *nothing* to help her. And what about Angel and Maria—where were they? Now where would they go? What about all those people who were trapped or dying? "No!" he screamed again.

The bedroom door opened quickly. His mother gathered him into her arms.

Joshua dropped his head on her shoulder. The scent of his father's pipe wafted from the flannel robe she had thrown over her nightgown. Unable to control the sudden torrent of tears, Joshua let himself be rocked like a little boy.

"Shh," whispered his mother as she stroked his hair. "Everything will be all right, sweetheart." She tried to hum a lullaby, but Joshua could tell she was weeping, too.

"I couldn't help Mrs. DiPietro," he wailed. "She died right there, holding on to my hand."

"But you *did* help Mrs. DiPietro, Josh. You comforted her. You sang for her. You made her passing sweet."

Joshua wondered vaguely how she knew what had happened.

"And here's some *good* news about your friend, Angel," Mom went on. "Marc sold Angel's drawing to the paper for a *hundred* dollars! The *Traveler* and Mr. Fitzgerald are sponsoring an art scholarship for her. Things are going to work out just fine for Angel and her sister."

Joshua pulled away from his mother. "You found out about . . . *everything?*"

Mom nodded. "Marc and Aunt Caroline told me all about it last night. I feel so bad that you had such a burden on your shoulders because of me." Tears spilled down her cheeks. "You thought I'd be *ashamed* that you were a newsboy."

"I'm sorry, Mom. Please don't cry."

"No, *I'm* sorry, Josh." She clutched Joshua into her arms again. "I'm so proud of you, Joshua. You risked your life to help that woman."

Joshua and his mother clung together as the morning sun slowly rose and drifted through the window.

Then Joshua remembered his papers. "I've got to get to town. I have a hundred papers to sell."

"Not today, Joshua. Forget about the papers. Listen, Mr. Williams called yesterday and said he may have a buyer for our land in Revere. Then you won't need to work anymore. We'll get a smaller house in the suburbs. You can go back to school, and"—she smiled—"and Aunt Caroline said she'd come with us!"

"That would be nice," Joshua said. "I love Aunt

Caroline." He stood up. "But now I've got to go into town. There's something I have to do." He couldn't explain to his mother why he had such a strong need to get back to the newspapers. He didn't understand it himself.

"All right, dear. If you feel you must, Josh." She got up to leave the room, then paused. "Marc isn't here. We had a long talk, and he went back to the newspaper. He stayed at the office all night writing about the molasses tragedy."

"Why did the tank explode?" Joshua asked.

"They don't really know yet. They think it had to do with the sudden change in the weather. Try not to think about it anymore, sweetheart. I'll get your breakfast." She left the room, and Joshua could hear her talking softly to Aunt Caroline.

Later, on the rattling El, people spoke in excited voices about the "Great Molasses Flood." Everyone had different ideas of what had caused the tank to rupture.

Joshua watched the buildings speed by. It was hard to believe that yesterday had happened at all. Remembering was painful—like a frightful dream. His hands smarted from where the glass had cut him, reminding him that it hadn't been a dream at all.

Joshua got off at Newspaper Alley. The *Traveler* building was bursting with reporters and newsboys. Here, too, the Great Molasses Flood was the only topic of discussion. How had it happened? Who was to blame?

Joshua looked around for Charlie, but didn't see him.

As Joshua piled his papers onto a cart, he read the headlines. The word **"EXTRA!"** was stamped on the front page.

**"TRAGEDY IN BOSTON'S NORTH END,"** read the headlines. **"MOLASSES TANK EXPLODES! 2,300,000 GALLONS OF MOLASSES KILL TWENTY-ONE SOULS. FIFTY MORE SERIOUSLY INJURED. GIANT WALL OF MOLASSES CRUSHES EVERYTHING IN ITS PATH."** The byline read: by Marc Muggeridge, Editor.

Joshua figured Marc must be happy to have made this big scoop. But surely not at the expense of so many lives? Marc had not looked happy when Joshua saw him at the site of the disaster.

Reporting is his job, Joshua decided. How else would people know what others were going through? How else could they help?

Charlie was waiting for Joshua on State Street. "You made it," he said quietly.

"Yep. I made it. Where are Angel and Maria? Are they okay?"

"Angel and Maria spent the night at my house. They're broke up about their mama, but their dad is on his way from Rhode Island to get them and take them to Providence. He's got a new job with his brother. Somethin' to do with designin' jewelry. Angel says he's a good artist."

"That must be where Angel gets her talent."

Charlie kicked a stone off the sidewalk. "She's grateful to you for stayin' with her ma."

"A lot of good I was. I couldn't do anything to help her."

"You *did* help her." Charlie punched Joshua lightly on the shoulder. "Now, you gotta come with me. I got somethin' to show you."

"I don't have time, Charlie. The papers will sell like crazy today."

"Leave your papes in the alley and follow me," Charlie ordered.

"Where are we going?" Joshua asked, trying to keep up with Charlie's rapid stride.

Charlie just waved him on with his hand and headed down Milk Street, stopping abruptly in front of the Custom House. Charlie stomped up the granite stairs as if he owned the place. Joshua followed.

In the front lobby an open elevator waited. "Hurry up, Charlie," said a uniformed man at the elevator controls. "I'm not supposed to be doin' this for you newspaper kids."

"I never asked a favor from ya before, but this here is somethin' special," Charlie said.

"Get in, then. Quick." The man shut the filigreed cage-like door and pulled the lever. Joshua's ears crackled as the elevator climbed, then finally stopped.

"Here y'are. The nineteenth floor," said the elevator operator. "You'll have to walk up the rest of the way." He pointed to a stairway. "I'll pick you up here in a half hour. Don't ring the bell."

"Come on," said Charlie.

The boys hiked the winding stairs to the twenty-sixth floor. Then, puffing from the climb, Charlie and Joshua pushed through the heavy doors to the observation deck.

"This here's the tippity top of Beantown," Charlie announced.

The weather had turned bitter cold and the frigid wind took Joshua's breath away. Even up here, the pungent smell of molasses mingled in the salty air.

Joshua stepped over to the railing. "Look down there, Charlie! The automobiles and wagons—and all those people scurrying around—why, they look just like windup penny toys."

"This is like bein' in one of them darned aeroplanes, ain't it?" Charlie yelled over the wind.

"We're above the clocks!"

"We're on the top, all right. Can't go much higher than this." Charlie pointed to the north. "See how the harbor is full of molasses?"

The once blue water was now eerie shades of brown and yellow. Near the gaping hole in the skyline where the molasses tank had been, Joshua could see plumes of water arching from fireboats as they sprayed salt water onto the wharves and streets. Fire engines on the land were spraying, too.

Joshua walked around to the side of the tower that faced the west.

As the morning sun grew brighter, lights in buildings flashed on and off, reminding Joshua of fireflies. The ice-laden Charles River wound its way to the open sea. When spring came, it would be dotted with sailboats. In the distance Joshua could see the graceful outline of the snow-covered New Hampshire foothills.

"It's just like you said, Dad," Joshua whispered. "The city is beautiful from this tower." He turned to Charlie. "How come you brought me up here?"

"It was Angel's idea," Charlie replied. "She said it's somethin' you always wanted."

"Yeah, it is," said Joshua. "Thanks, Charlie."

Charlie walked Joshua back to State Street. Joshua tried unsuccessfully, with his bandaged hands, to untie the cord that bound his pile of papers.

"Here, lemme do it," Charlie said, pulling out a

jackknife. "Have you read the papes yet?" he asked as he cut the string.

"I read Marc's story about the tank."

"Well, you oughtta take a look at the *second page*. There's somethin' there you need to see."

Joshua opened one of the papers to page two.

## A SONG IN THE CITY

### BY MARC MUGGERIDGE

Yesterday, amidst the anguish and pain that filled our city, there was one moment of peace, faith, and hope when a song rang out over the scene of devastation.

As Mrs. Rosa DiPietro was fatally injured and barely clinging to life, a brave newsboy stayed by her side in a crumbling tenement. Instead of fleeing as the building slowly collapsed, he took her hand and sang a hymn.

Although Mrs. DiPietro died from the injuries she sustained in the Great Molasses Flood, her final moments were brightened by the song and the beauty of the voice that floated across the field of destruction and strengthened all who heard it.

The newsboy sang—not only for Mrs. DiPietro, not only for the victims of the disaster, but for our entire city. His name, Joshua Harper.

Joshua was stunned. "How did Marc know I sang to Mrs. DiPietro?" he asked.

"Everyone heard you, kid! Your voice rang out like a darned bell."

Joshua looked away. "I didn't know what else to do. Mrs. DiPietro wanted me to pray. I don't know how to pray for Catholics."

"What you did was fine. It was the *right* thing. Hey, you wanna know what one woman said? She said there was an angel there singin' after the tragedy." Charlie laughed. "Yep, she thought *you* were an angel. O' course, *I* know better. You ain't no angel, but you're a real hero, kid. And you have the voice of an angel to boot." Unexpectedly, Charlie threw both arms around Joshua and hugged him. Then, just as quickly, he pulled himself away. "You better get busy sellin' those papes. People will be expectin' to hear you singin' your city song." He clapped his hand on Joshua's shoulder before heading up the sidewalk.

Joshua watched Charlie disappear around the corner at Washington Street. Then, holding up a newspaper, Joshua inhaled deeply—and sang out the day's headlines.

# HISTORICAL NOTE

Yes! It really did happen! The most bizarre tragedy that ever took place in Boston, Massachusetts, was the "Great Molasses Flood" of January 15, 1919, yet it is rarely referred to in history books. A 55-foot-high steel tank containing 2 1/2 million gallons of crude molasses burst open, causing a giant tidal wave of molasses that deluged everything in its path. Some folks joke about "the sticky situation" this event caused. However, this disaster killed 21 people and injured 150 others, some of whom died later from their injuries.

Cleanup took a long time. Boston Harbor itself was brown for six months. And it's not easy to wash molasses from cobblestone streets! Fresh water didn't work, so they sprayed seawater all over the area.

Although my story is fiction, the scenes that take

place are based upon fact. The *rat-a-tat* of breaking rivets; the sucking cyclone of wind; the thirty-five-to-fifty-foot-high tidal wave as it descended upon the North End community; the broken trestle of the elevated train really happened. Some articles say that the El train screeched to a stop *after* the flood. Others say it passed safely by just *before* the flood.

Buildings were crushed by the wave of molasses. The fire station was lifted off its foundation and carried to the very edge of the harbor. The deadly thick goo filled basements, and as the buildings and tenements crumbled around them, victims—people and animals—fell into the churning gluey mess and drowned. One man was swept into the harbor and was later rescued. Children on their way home from school were caught in the molasses. Disaster pelted from the sky, too, as jagged chunks of the shattered tank flew like shell fire in a war. One boy suffered a fractured skull from a catapulting steel fragment.

Some of the people in my story were real. Anthony di Stasio did get swept up by the molasses on his way home from school—and lived to tell about it. But his little sister was killed in the flood. Officer McManus was at his police call box when the tank exploded, and his call for help is part of the story. Bridget Clougherty was killed when she was blown through the wall of her brick house at the foot of Copps Hill. Even poor Peter, the tiger cat, actually existed—and died in the flood.

What caused the tank to explode? The official cause was determined to be the tank's structural weakness, including an insufficient number of rivets and poor quality steel, plus the fact it had recently been filled to capacity. The weather in Boston had been cold for several days, with temperatures down in the single digits. Then a "January thaw" rapidly brought the temperature up to about 40 degrees Fahrenheit. With the sudden changes in outside temperatures, the expansion and contraction of the molasses caused the tank to blow apart.

A conflicting account says the tank contained steam pipes that warmed its contents, so it could be poured easily into tank cars and transported to nearby Cambridge for processing. When overheated, molasses ferments and exudes a highly volatile gas. Some experts feel this gas ignited, creating the deadly explosion. If this was the cause, it would explain some references to the molasses being "boiling hot." Also, some stories say, "If the molasses didn't drown you, it would cook you!" However, other accounts by victims do not mention the molasses being hot. Some authorities believe this rumor was spread by police to keep people away from the scene of the disaster.

Other parts of this story are based on fact. The Great Influenza Epidemic, also known as the "Spanish Influenza," was the most devastating plague in history. Boston, Massachusetts, and the nearby army base, Fort Devens, were among the first American communities to contract the deadly disease. The plague began in September 1918, and lasted less than a year, killing an estimated *40 million people* worldwide!

Boston's famous Custom House Tower was the city's first skyscraper. It is listed with the National Register of Historic Places. Visitors can now ride elevators all the way up to the observation deck to enjoy the view.

Many of the newsboys and bootblacks in 1919 Boston were spoken of as "boys in men's shoes" since they took on responsibilities for their families by working long hours and often sacrificing their own education. Girls were also among this group. Foundations and scholarships were set up for the newsboys and bootblacks, and some of these young people grew up to become lawyers, publishers, and musicians. A picture from one of the foundations for newsboys shows an older newsboy comforting a younger one, saying, "Never mind, Jimmie, tomorrow you'll sell all your papers."

Boston's Mayor John Fitzgerald, the grandfather of President John F. Kennedy, was at one time a Boston newsboy. The experiences he relates to Joshua in the story are true. And it was Mayor Fitzgerald who established the North End Playground, where part of the story takes place.

The snowball fight on the Boston Common was a custom for many years when the "highbrow" Beacon Street boys would fight in the park with the poor Irish and Italian gangs from the North End of the city.

The historic North End of Boston is where you'll find the home of Paul Revere and the Old North Church, where the signal was given on April 18, 1775, for the minutemen to spread the warning "The British are coming!" at the time of the American Revolution.

At the foot of Copps Hill, a skating rink and park have replaced the gloomy area where the molasses flood actually took place. The quaint North End neighborhoods and the Copps Hill Burial Ground are great places to visit—and to enjoy the Italian restaurants that line the narrow streets.

The Great Molasses Flood is sometimes portrayed as a humorous chapter of Boston history. I hope, after reading my story, you will remember the incident as it really was: a preventable tragedy that destroyed many innocent lives.

If you visit Boston, Massachusetts, on a summer day, close your eyes and sniff the air. It is said that on hot days the smell of molasses still rises from beneath the Boston streets.

# ACKNOWLEDGMENTS

Many, many thanks to:

Nancy McCue, Jane Rice, and Sue Stokes, at the Moultonboro, New Hampshire Public Library—my "summer" library—who can find information on just about anything; Ann Lieberman and the Reference Department at the Venice, Florida, Public Library—my "winter" library; Robyn Christensen, at the Bostonian Society Library, who supplied me with much of the historical data and photographs regarding the Great Molasses Flood; and the Boston Public Library's online resource program.

Much appreciation to Charles Parrott, National Park Service Historical Architect, who provided facts about old Boston and its first skyscraper, the Custom House Tower.

Thank you to Ellen Silverman, Chef Concierge; Karen Connors, Concierge; and Mark Harrington, Security Supervisor at Marriott's Custom House, for a spectacular tour of the Custom House Tower and its breathtaking view.

For critique, moral support, and friendship, I am grateful to my Sarasota, Florida, writing group: Carol Behrman, June Fiorelli, Gail Hedrick, and Elizabeth Wall.

A million megabytes of thanks to my cousin, Hugh Small, who, in his passion to dig up online history, unearthed fascinating details about Boston's "sticky" past.

*Ciao!* and *Mille grazie!* to my dear friends Elena and Ed Morse for help with Italian dialogue.

To Emma Dryden, my inspiring editor, who believed in this story, thank you!

And to Debbie, Lisa, Kristan, Scott, and Jennifer, my captive audience, who cheer me on in innumerable ways, I send more thanks and love than all the beans in Boston!